You are
Forever in
My Heart

Happy Reading,
Love,

You are Forever in My Heart

SANJEEV RANJAN

Srishti
PUBLISHERS & DISTRIBUTORS

SRISHTI PUBLISHERS & DISTRIBUTORS
Registered Office: N-16, C.R. Park
New Delhi – 110 019
Corporate Office: 212A, Peacock Lane
Shahpur Jat, New Delhi – 110 049
editorial@srishtipublishers.com

First published by
Srishti Publishers & Distributors in 2018

To all lovely and beautiful couples
in the world, who keep my belief
in love and relationships intact.

*The greatest tragedy of human life is when
your heart longs for love and there
is no one around to love you.*

Author's note and acknowledgement

I have written this book after a long gap of almost three years. This book is very close to my heart and it was an emotional journey for me to write down each incident, going back into the past and feeling every emotion and then portraying it on paper. I wasn't sure if I could do justice to it, but this story needed to be told. As I also mentioned in all my earlier books, I reiterate that writing a book is a long and arduous journey in itself, which cannot be completed alone. It's true for this book as well. There are several great people who accompanied me during this journey and made it smooth during the frustrating times. I want to thank them heartily.

To begin with, thanks to my mom and dad who supported me throughout, encouraged me, and gave me the freedom to do what I wanted to do. My brother and sister, thanks to you both for being a part of this journey.

To my dear friend Vineet – thank you for being a strong pillar of support, for tolerating my eccentricities, bearing my frustrations, listening to my useless chatter for hours without interrupting me when things looked too dark, for reading a few chapters and giving feedback, and empowering me through my rough days despite your tight schedule.

Special thanks to my dear friend Rishabh, for showing confidence in me and encouraging me all the time. Your words – "Sanjeev, I know you can do it" – always motivated me.

Stuti Sharma – thank you for your careful, wise and razor-sharp editing. Also for sorting out all my genuine or vague queries, and making the process smoother for me. Thanks to the entire team at Srishti Publishers for helping me at every stage of publishing.

I want to express my gratitude to all my lovely readers who bought my books, read them, and took pains to connect with me on social media or through emails. I thank you from the bottom of my heart. It is your love and affection that were pillars of support to me during these years.

Lastly, my deepest and most sincere thanks to all of you who remain connected with me and have faith in me. You can continue sending in your love at sanjeev.ranjan91@gmail.com.

Prologue

It was seemingly very pleasant for me. Probably the most important day of my life, I thought looking out of the window. The air itself seemed to be singing a melody for me, a known voice all around me, whispering to me, making me realize her presence. After all, I was releasing my next novel after a long break of five years. Not just that, this was the first time I was launching the book in such a grand fashion and coming face to face with my readers. This time, unlike the first, was totally different. The book was already the talk of the town and my publisher's best efforts in creating an initial buzz about the book seemed to have hit the nail on the head. The book had received rave reviews in several newspapers and magazines. Since a lot of readers were to be present at the launch, I was excited, yet nervous. The marketing and publicity teams had left no stone unturned to make the event successful and had booked the central space in the middle of the most popular shopping mall in Delhi for the launch. Simultaneously, social media platforms had been bombarded with interesting teasers, thought-provoking posters and romantic videos of the book to catch the readers' eyes. To get maximum readership, the book was listed for pre-order at every bookstore and online stores two months before the actual release of the book.

The event was to start at 7:30 p.m. and I had visited it around 5.30 p.m. just to have a look. It was huge and was decorated aptly for the event. Posters had been put up across the mall and a stage was ready with a huge banner at the back. I could see excited fans rushing in and securing a good place near the stage even two hours prior to the event. The staff working behind the scene had estimated a turn-up of around two hundred and fifty people; but the situation half an hour before the launch said otherwise. Just when I had reached the hotel close to the mall to get ready, one of the team members called up to tell me that all the chairs had been taken and there were a good amount of people standing at the back. The crowd was expected to cross five hundred.

I had goose bumps. I had been told that a celebrity was to launch the book, though it was kept as a surprise for me too. Lest I get disappointed in the event of things not going as per plan.

I wanted to prepare myself before I appeared in front of so many people. I didn't want to disappoint anyone – neither with my book, nor with my appearance. I modified the speech that I had written five years back when I had written my first book. Though there hadn't been any book launch back then, I had kept the speech safe nonetheless. Being an introvert who shied away from readers, I had never appeared in front of them and had never organized any kind of formal ceremony to launch the book. Despite maintaining a low profile in the public sphere, I had always been on my toes, replying to their emails or posts on social media. But when it came to a face to face conversation,

I always found it tough to handle questions, because I was a writer by chance. I had written down my heart and it had become a story.

I looked at the speech one last time, closed my eyes to calm myself down and looked at myself in the mirror for the Nth time. The pair of jeans I wore with a contrasting shirt and a blazer looked fine. My publisher had briefed me that at launches such as these, readers don't come to talk of the book. They would all be coming to listen to me, chat with me and to know what I had in my heart but hadn't revealed in the book.

Time was passing. The phone buzzed, flashing a message from Ruchita.

Come soon. I have already reached the venue. The crowd looks fantastic and excited. ☺

I smiled reading the message. Before I called for the cab, I looked at the photo frame kept on the table, pulled it closer and kissed the picture.

I reached the venue in just about ten minutes. I was greeted by the cheer of the crowd. I couldn't believe it was for me. I saw Ruchita in the front row, cheering for me. I waved at her to acknowledge her presence, but in turn, all the readers who had seen me waving, waved back at me. Almost three hundred people had gathered there and the space around it was abuzz with my posters and their chatter. The organizers had already put up innumerable copies of the book on the stage and around it. Most of the readers had already got their copies. It was a huge crowd. It filled my heart with love for them and I waved my hand at them and smiled. They smiled, cheered, hooted and called out my name, waving back at me. It was surreal; almost magical.

My publisher was there too, and the marketing manager took me backstage. I met everyone who had helped make the

event so successful and expressed my gratitude. I was soon
guided to occupy a seat on the stage along with my editor who
had encouraged me to write this book.

On the table kept in front of us, I could see three gift-
wrapped books, perhaps the ones to be unveiled in front of the
crowd. There were also bottles of mineral water and a mike. A
mere look at the mike made my throat go dry with nervousness.
But all the time, I was smiling looking at the excited readers.
Whatever I was today, it was all because of them.

We could hear a commotion at the entrance of the mall.
The anchor on stage announced that we had a well-known
author amidst us, who would be unveiling the book along with
me. When he came up on the stage, we shook hands and he
mentioned how he had loved my style of writing and the story.

The anchor took the mike and introduced us, along with
describing the occasion. When asked to open the gift wrap,
I joked that I hoped it was my book inside. There was mild
laughter from the audience.

I could easily hear the loud cheering when I unveiled the
book. I was asked to speak a few words when the cheering had
subsided. This was a very special moment for me. I picked up
the mike and looked at the crowd. There was absolute silence, as
if they couldn't wait to hear me. For a long moment, I remained
silent. My heart was overwhelmed with emotions; only I knew
how difficult this journey of writing this book had been. For a
moment, I closed my eyes, feeling everything in me and said
slowly:

"We collect our experiences and put together our
circumstances into stories…stories we pick up along the way
and carry with us."

There was a constant rhythm of applause, as memories flashed in front of my eyes. I continued, "And this story is the result of those circumstances that have shaped my life. It's deep in my heart and I have made it immortal in the pages of my book.

L ife is funny. It reminds me of Bono's song: '*There is no end to grief, there is no end to love.*'

Has it ever happened with you? That you lay down in your cosy bed at the end of a long day and lose yourself to thoughts? All kinds of thoughts. When your heart wanted to scream and cry, but no voice came out, fearing it would wake everyone else up. Rather scare them in the dead of the night. So, you just lay there, watching the ceiling fan as if it held the answers to all your dilemmas, and let the pain break you.

This is how I spent most of my nights. Actually, every single night. I would return from office to an empty house, let the office bag slide onto the floor near the foot of the bed and slouch in bed myself, drowning in the sea of memories, the black hole of loneliness.

Sometime in the middle of my stint with my thoughts and memories, the doorbell would ring twice. That's the boy who delivered my dinner in a tiffin. I would eat as much as was necessary to survive and pick my phone up. It was a ritual for me to scroll through my contacts list. Clearly, I wanted to talk to someone who cared about me. Though my Dad called me around 9:00 p.m. every day to ask how I was, and talked for a few seconds before hanging up, it was more like a routine for me to go through than a chance to open up my heart. In the end, I could never find any names in my contacts list on which I could click to call. I would then scroll through WhatsApp, check my Facebook notifications and Gmail. I would read the messages, and accept friend requests from unknown people. It was an attempt to pass time which otherwise moved at snail's pace, making it impossible for me to do anything meaningful.

That fateful day, it was around 10:30 p.m. when I went to bed. Like every night, I stared at the fan and thought of the past days, weeks and months. I tried meditating, hoping it would soothe the pain that my heart battled single-handedly, but the many muffled voices inside my head drove me crazy. Like every other night, I felt an urge to read those old conversations that once had been the foundation of my existence. And every time I read it, I felt nostalgic about the past and inevitably became sad.

I had always been a loner, even as a child. But now I was lonely, and not by choice. Deep in my heart, I knew that nobody else would be able to help me if I did not do something about it myself. So I tried to blend in with the world and be social. But the more people I met, the more disappointed I was. Everyone was so self-absorbed that I felt like an intruder, almost unwanted in their space. So I stopped expecting anything from anyone. I wanted to be self-sufficient, not having to depend on anyone in the world for anything. Not even my parents and family.

Trying to find a way out of my pain, I picked up the novel that I had been trying to finish reading for the last one month. I flipped through the pages and started reading random sections. In the myriad emotions that I felt, I didn't realize when my eyes closed and I drifted off to sleep.

"I love you," I was saying to someone.

"I love you too, baby," a sweet voice answered.

Then everything suddenly went blank. As if it was a black hole and whatever had been happening till now had been erased. It was dark everywhere, and like a sudden ray of light she appeared again, smiling, wearing the red suit that I had always loved on her. She looked like a princess out of a fairy tale, who I had been waiting for all my life. Every time I saw her, I fell in love with her...all over again. My love for her grew manifold with every second that passed, making her an inseparable part of my life. Though I was standing a few steps away from her, my eyes followed her wherever she went. When she entered the class, she smiled, and my face lit up like a child's when given a chocolate.

It was Valentine's Day. We had wished each other at midnight, and when we met on the roof of my house the next evening, we wished each other again, this time exchanging countless kisses... some long, some mere pecks. The moment was made more romantic by the rain that suddenly drenched us.

"It's raining!" I said.

"Yeah, isn't it so romantic? Just imagine...you and me, alone on the roof and rain. Our clothes glued to our skin," she smiled wickedly, now completely drenched. Her clothes were sticking to her, showing bits of her that I had not yet seen.

"And we come closer looking into each other's eyes...And then, an abrupt burst of thunder and lightning makes me jump onto you. Cling to you out of fear. Our lips are an inch away and you put your puffy lips on mine. Our warm breath would make the ambience even more romantic. We'd kiss perfectly and passionately for a long time."

I was amazed at how she had narrated the whole scene, also giving me a glimpse into what she wanted from me. "Give me a kiss," she said, smiling broadly. She leaned towards me and I could sense she was teasing me.

"Are you mad? Here? Everyone can see us. It's the terrace, not my room. No way." My eyes popped out in astonishment.

"At least on my cheek," she said and chuckled.

"You are out of your mind. If you insist, I will have to go," I warned, trying to sound harsh. It wasn't of any use, because she was smiling all through, as if daring me.

"See, there's no one around here, not even a single soul. Now you have no excuse."

The romance blacked out suddenly, just like a movie had been stopped in the middle. It was totally dark when her voice resonated in the background. It was not sweet anymore.

"Just get lost and never try to contact me!"

I woke up startled, the last line of the dream playing like a murderous loop in my mind. The words drowning me in pain as much as I was soaked in sweat. I was out of breath, panting. I looked around and hurriedly picked up a bottle of water from the bedside table. I gulped the water down as if it could save me from dying. After I became stable in about a couple of minutes, I checked the phone. It flashed 5:30 a.m.

It was common for me to wake up this way. My nights would be clouded with memories, and days began with searing pain after such dreams. There was nothing I could do about it, except asking myself over and over – why did it happen with me? It had been years now, but the memories were as fresh as the past moment. Why couldn't I forget her even after so many years? Even when I had penned every single thought and feeling I felt for her on paper in the form of a book. I had hoped things would be fine after the book, but it hadn't helped much and dreams of her continued to haunt me.

My inner demons tortured me. "How could she do this to me? She cheated on me. She made fun of my love." A wistful pain swept through my heart. "Loyalty...my love for her and all my goodness. She played with it." The pain took the form of tears and rolled down my cheeks. "I loved her so much. I apologized for a crime that I didn't even know I had committed. I said sorry a million times. I even pleaded with her to stay in my life. Told her I could not live without her. She was stone-hearted to not have seen my heart bleeding."

A few years back, I had fallen in love with Ashima. It was magical; as if we were pieces of a puzzle waiting to be put together. I was sure she was the one I was looking for, the love of my life. It was dreamy like the movies, and Ashima was no less than a princess for me. I wanted to spend each moment of my life with her, revelling in the love and romance that kindled our spirits.

But like every love story, my love story also turned sour with time. The romance changed to bickering, and we both started fighting with each other over silly issues. Things changed rapidly after that and I began feeling that I wasn't her priority anymore. She always came first in my life, but I seemed to be in a queue; waiting for my share of attention amidst a million distractions. It was a feeling I hated deeply. After that, it didn't take long for things to turn ugly between us. I also found out that she was cheating on me. Fights and bickering is alright, but how could she cheat on me! I had given her everything I could, and for what! To be stabbed in the back like this? To see her roaming around with another man and ignoring me to give him her time.

The pain overwhelmed me, and since I didn't have anyone who I could share it with, it kept growing, not finding a vent. Initially, when I was unable to come to terms with the pain in my heart, I used to scribble my thoughts on any stray piece of paper that I could lay hands on. Even on paper napkins that cafes offer with the food. At times these were little romantic brushes, and at others the sad little things of the heart that could not be explained or told.

The story that I had lived for a few months took an entire year to be penned down in the diary. If you think it was easy to live all those memories again, without her by my side this time, you're mistaken. I remained aloof most of the time, tortured by memories that surrounded me. Sometimes, to clear my mind, I used to walk in the college campus in the evenings, alone. My life seemed caught in the rut – classroom to my room, and from my room to the classroom. I hardly talked to anyone, not even my roommates. They tried to bring me back into their world, but it was of no use. They thought I was arrogant or haughty, perhaps. I wish I could tell them why I had become like that.

I wanted others to read my story too, maybe then they would understand me better. But I never thought of sharing it with anyone else. Not yet. And, after an entire year of scribbling and writing, cutting and rewriting, putting down words as had been shared between me and her, and battling my emotions, I finished writing. It was as if my heart had directly poured out the venom that had been taking my life away slowly.

Whoever said tears don't have weight was absolutely wrong. When tears roll down, the heart becomes lighter. And in writing the book, I had shed plenty of tears. Though hiding from my roommates, lest I became the butt of their ridicule and gossip.

I had thought writing it all out would take the pain away. But I was wrong. One can't escape from memories so easily. If it would have been the case, there would have been no sorrow in this world.

During my engineering days, out of the three friends with whom I used to spend some time, Rishabh was quite observant. He used to keep looking at me from the corner of his eye. I won't lie, but it used to creep me out initially. Eventually I learnt to ignore it. One evening, he was alone in the room while I had gone out for my customary lonely walk. He must have seen my diary lying on the bedside table and didn't hesitate to read it. When I came back, he was smiling at me. Just when I was about to turn around and go my way, I noticed my diary in his hands.

"So this is where you've been busy all these days! You finished it, man! Nailed it,' Rishabh said animatedly.

I was angry that he had read it without asking me, but pleased that someone had finally read it. "Yes," I said with a sad smile.

"I am sorry I didn't ask you, but I read a few pages. Randomly, you know. It's interesting. Ever thought of getting it published?"

"Published? Have you had a bet with someone to humour me? This is just the rambling of a sad heart. And I have written it for my personal catharsis. I'm sure not one publishing house would be interested in this crap," I said sitting on my bed and looking out of the window, avoiding his gaze. After all, he was the first one to have glimpsed into my sadness.

"You can at least try. In fact, my father was telling me about someone in the family who is a freelance editor. If you fear the book doesn't read that well right now, take an expert's opinion. Or get the book edited if you wish."

I was deep in my thoughts, and didn't want any suggestions just then. "Okay, I will think about it. Thanks."

Rishabh returned my diary, patted my back with an encouraging smile, and headed to the mess for dinner, but I stayed back. I was staring at the ceiling fan again, thinking.

'Who would want to publish a college student's tears,' my head argued. My heart said, 'Everyone lives through the same life with the same set of feelings. Someone somewhere will find something in the story that touches their heart.' It was confusing, but I sat up on my bed and pulled the laptop out of my bag lying next to the bed. I Googled leading publishers in the city and read their requirements. Somewhere in the middle, it started looking foolish to me and I shut the machine down, before pulling the bed sheet over my face.

It took me almost two years to find a publisher willing to publish my story, and that too after fifteen rejections.

Not much had changed in the past two years, but the pain had somehow befriended me. It didn't hurt as much now. And I had found a friend too. Rishabh would cheer me up, coax me into joining others. But I was happy with myself, and he never forced me. The book finally got published when I was in the last semester of my course. Since I did not have many friends, I kept it to myself. I didn't want unnecessary attention anyway. Others came to know about it when Rishabh tagged me on Facebook and declared that I was an author. People wished me luck, but nobody bought the book, except Rishabh. Just after the release of the book, he bought a copy, read it and came to my room to get it autographed. Students had warned Rishabh about spending time with me; they thought he would also go crazy like me and no one would talk to him. I didn't know if Rishabh was going crazy; but he was learning to ignore people for sure.

Even though I hadn't promoted the book much, soon I started receiving emails from readers. My heart felt content when readers said they found the story deeply emotional, and a few of them said that they could connect well with the story. I was active on Facebook, Twitter and various other platforms when it came to connecting with my readers, because their feedback gave me happiness.

College ended soon after, and I shifted to Delhi for my job. Even at my workplace, I never once mentioned my book. I am guessing, but a few colleagues came to know about it through social media. They used to say, "You are a celebrity. How many copies has the book sold so far? How much money have you earned so far?"

There were times when I chose to not answer, because the book was a labour of love, not a means to make money! Again, I was adjudged as an arrogant person. I accepted this tag as my fate and started believing that I was different. The only time I connected with my colleagues was over some team discussion, out of professional courtesy.

Among all my colleagues, only Kavya got curious about my book when she came to know about it from someone else in the office. She had joined the office a few months after me. One morning she came and told me she had read my book, and loved it. She looked ever so happy to have met an author in person.

That same afternoon, I was checking my mails when I saw a fan's message after a very long time. It was from a young girl named Shuchi.

Dear Sanjeev,

My name is Shuchi and I'm a second year student at Delhi University. I finished reading your novel, **In Course of True Love,** *just about five minutes back. I picked it up at a bookstore because I loved the cover. Now, after finishing the book, I couldn't stop myself from mailing you.*

I love the way you have revealed yourself in the name of Aarush. From the beginning, I felt that it is the reality of your life that you have tried to share with people. Your love for the girl made me cry, and I think you still love her and will continue to care for her.

I feel the world is strange; those who give ample unconditional love never get as much in return.

I want you to reply to this email. I will keep waiting. I so want to meet you. If you ever come to Delhi, please let me know.

P.S. I am in love with Aarush. I find him very cute.

With love,

Shuchi

It made me smile.

I always replied to readers, and this girl had guessed that it was my story. I typed an email expressing my gratitude and assured her that if I ever came to Delhi, I would definitely let her know and meet her. I knew I was lying to her as I was already in Delhi. I didn't want to meet anyone. Just as I hit the send button, Kavya called me from behind, a copy of my novel in her hand.

"Who are you chit chatting with, Mr Author?" said Kavya, jovially.

"Was just replying to a reader's email," I said casually, turning towards her.

"Wow! They write to you? Daily?" asked Kavya.

"Not daily. But yes, sometimes. And it feels nice."

"That's wonderful. I am glad you take out time to reply. It would definitely make them happy." She wore a broad smile, and I also returned one, although milder. "It must be a wonderful feeling to see a mail or message from a fan, no?" she continued.

"It feels good, no doubt," I said and changed the topic of the conversation. "What's that in your hands?" I asked, although I knew very well what it was.

"Oh, yes!" She glanced at it and said, "I brought it along with me today to get your autograph. I love author signed copies."

I signed the copy for her. After Rishabh, Kavya was the only one to have asked for my autograph.

Our bonding flourished after that. Since we sat next to each other in office, we ended up talking to each other about various things. I often spent my time with her during lunch or over evening tea and she seemed to enjoy her time with me. She often talked about her boyfriend who never reciprocated the same feelings for her as she did for him. At times when we didn't have much workload, we just sneaked out and walked around the office campus, talking about relationships. She often asked me what had happened with Ashima, or if I had tried to contact her again, but I always refused to answer or changed the topic.

She eventually secured a better paying job in Bangalore and resigned from the job in the next two months. With a smiling face, we bid adieu to each other and I was left alone again. With nobody to talk to in office now, I also decided to move on and resigned from the company. I also got a job in a start-up. I hoped young employees in the new office would kick start my life too and bring back my smile.

I was yet to join the new office and my notice period at the previous one had ended. I was left with a lot of free time. It had been several months since I had interacted with any of my friends. I didn't feel like meeting anyone either. Though Rishabh had tried calling me many a time, I never picked up. I uninstalled WhatsApp from my phone and was even tempted to delete all profiles on social media. But my readers and their feedback was the only thing keeping me sane. I couldn't have let go of that.

People came and left, but my dreams continuously disturbed my sleep. I wanted to say so much, but there was no one to listen to me. Honestly, I knew I had pushed a few people away, but my heart craved for just that one who had left me in this vortex of pain and suffering. Everyone else had the same dialogues – with time, things will be okay; this was just an affair, forget about it and move on! Few even suggested that I look for another girlfriend, but I was happier without such advice.

One evening, I was sulking alone in the room when the doorbell rang. Once, twice. I thought the boy with the tiffin had come in early. But the doorbell rang again, with a frequency that could raise even the dead. I wondered who it could be and went to open the door. The moment I opened the door, someone pounced upon me and held my collar. I was stunned at the sudden assault. When I finally opened my eyes, I saw Rishabh. He was fuming.

"Where the hell are you these days?"

"I am here only; where would I go?" I made a brief reply, closing the door.

"Then why the hell are you not taking my calls?"

"I don't feel like meeting or talking to anyone. Her dreams keep haunting me even after so many years. As if my brain has suffered the blow as much as my heart. I am feeling helpless and I don't know what to do," I said as I walked in and sat on the couch.

Rishabh shouted at me, perhaps for the first time. "You can't always use the 'breakup with Ashima' story as your reason for not coming out from this room or meeting any of us ever, Sanjeev! Do you realize how many times I have called you in the last week and the number of messages I have dropped? Did you bother to reply or call back? It has been four fucking years now. Why don't you enjoy your life again and move on?"

"What did you just say? I am using her as a reason? What do you know of my pain, Rishabh? She has killed a part of me when she left me. And I don't understand what you mean by enjoying life. I don't like doing anything, you understand? I feel comfortable in this room, doing my daily activities. I don't feel like talking to anyone, not even you. You know why? Because you all keep asking the same questions over and over…like you were asking now. I don't want to answer your questions, you get it?" My voice had also started getting louder.

"You feel comfortable in this room! This goddamn room that you have turned into some kind of jail. Nothing seems to be at its right place. Look at the laundry bag! O gosh, how many days has it been that you have done the laundry? For god's sake, open your eyes and see what you're doing. You can't live and spend your life like this. You are wasting it. You have stopped reading books. I don't see any new books in this room. I even asked at the gym. You haven't visited the gym even once in the last three weeks. Your room stinks…and you are saying you are comfortable here…" and suddenly he stopped. His voice lowered and he whispered, "Wait a second! What the fuck is this?"

I turned around to see what he was talking about. He was looking at the wine bottle kept beside my bed and an ash tray with cigarette butts in it. He picked it up and walked towards me.

"Sanjeev, what the fuck is this? Since when did you start drinking and smoking?"

"Since last night," I said guiltily. I used to be the one dead against these abusive substances in college.

"Why? You remember how you were against it? You were ready to kill me once when I got drunk and passed out, remember?" he questioned me in quite an authoritative manner.

"I hadn't been able to sleep properly for the past few nights. So I bought the bottle of red wine. People say cigarettes with wine are a deadly combination, so I thought of giving it a shot. It's better than going crazy because of sleeplessness. And aah, I must say…people are right. Though I found it a bit difficult to smoke initially and hated the taste of the wine, but yes, I slept well after a long time. I didn't have any dream the entire night."

He became more furious at me. "Now you want her to be the reason to drink and smoke too! Very good! Alright, if you have decided to ruin yourself like this, I have also decided. I am going to inform your mom."

He took out his phone and started dialling some number. I thought he was kidding, perhaps to threaten me or something, but he was serious about it. It angered me and I shouted, "Stop it! Who are you calling anyway? Mom? Whose mom? That woman who never cared about me? People say she gave birth to me, but I am convinced she is my step-mother. You know, it has been three years that I have spoken to her. If you call her, she will most likely ask you who Sanjeev is. Maybe for you and for others, a mother symbolizes the epitome of kindness and love; but it isn't the same for me. For me, she has failed as a mother; and I have failed as a son. Ashima was the one filling up this gap in my life and then she also left. Asked me to go away. Cheated on me! Like my mother. Now you know why I am so emotionally broken? Perhaps now you know why no one can fix it."

None of us spoke for a few minutes. But whatever I said did not stop him. "Whatever reasons you give to justify your pain and anguish, I won't let you become a drunkard who is hell bent on ruining his life. I don't care if things don't work out between you and your mom. I care about you. And I know how much you love your dad. Have you ever thought how he would feel if he comes to know about all this? I am sure you don't want to hurt him."

"Okay, fine! You win. I won't drink or smoke again. But right now, you need to get out of this place."

His expressions changed rapidly. I knew was offended. After all, he had left everything and come to check on me, and here I was... asking him to get out.

"Fine!" he said, "I am leaving. But, I am telling you, you are wasting your life. Just try to remember how ambitious and energetic you were just about four years back. Think about your dreams, your life. And look at yourself now!" He walked towards the door and pulled it open with great force. He was at the threshold, but just before shutting the door behind him, he said something that shattered my broken world into a million pieces. "I don't know if this makes you feel better or makes it worse, but I got to know from someone that Ashima is with someone else and planning to marry him. She is living happily while you are killling yourself every moment. I think you should stop thinking about her and move on."

The door closed with a thud. He was gone, leaving me in a whirlpool of pain and confusion.

An unusual madness took over me. I don't know what I was thinking, but I hurriedly jumped towards my laptop and clicked open my Facebook account. I was sure she would have an account there. I searched her name, but her profile didn't appear. I even tried searching for her through her email id, but still no results. If Rishabh had come to know about it, it must have been through Facebook. I understood that she had blocked me. I logged out of the profile without checking the twenty odd friend requests and notifications. I didn't care about anything at that time. I forgot everything else, because Rishabh's words were killing me. My heartbeats were so loud, I could practically hear them.

I opened Gmail and clicked to register afresh. I created a fake email id and signed up on Facebook with this fake id. I hurriedly searched for her profile and found it. I checked the details available and found that she had been in a relationship for more than two years, with some engineer guy in a government office. Her profile was well protected to unknown users but I could still see some information and pictures. From whatever I saw, my heart sank with utmost sadness and I felt like crying. Seeing those pictures drove me insane.

I closed the laptop screen and changed into a clean t-shirt, the last clean t-shirt left in my wardrobe. I walked towards the nearest shop to get another bottle of wine. Even though I had promised Rishabh that I wouldn't drink anymore, I knew in my heart that this night would be the worst if I didn't have alcohol to my rescue. I came back with the bottle, opened her Facebook profile again and kept looking at her pictures. I had access to only two pictures, both with her new boyfriend. That night it took me an entire bottle of wine, and a whole lot of will power to pull out the wire of the laptop to stop seeing her pictures. I had imagined an entire lifetime with her, and now, it was so tough for me to look at her with someone else. I kept drowning myself in the wine little by little and kept crying.

I said to myself amidst sobs, "What has happened to me? Why am I not able to move on? Look, how happy she is with him, and look at me! I am sulking for her... who left me midway and didn't even look back. Does she even remember my name? I don't think so. Then why am I not able to forget her and live my life the way it should be lived." I stopped thinking, trying to clear my mind, but the sadness continued. "I don't find anything around me good. I need her. Nothing except her inspires me."

You know, I always wondered what love really is? What happens when one is in love? Love had come into my life after much waiting. The way they showed in the movies, love seemed like a beautiful thing, an adorable feeling. It makes your life complete; it shapes your life and gives you inspiration to live. A feeling which can't be measured, but can only be felt.

That's how I felt when she came into my life; like an angel to fill the void which I had always felt. In all the days that we were together, it looked like Ashima was the love that I had been waiting for all my life. I was happy that I'd share my emotions and feelings with someone who was so pure. I discovered an aspect of life that I was unaware of till then, a hidden beauty in the form of Ashima who loved me.

But after what she did to me, it seemed what I had thought about love was all wrong. But despite all that, not a single feeling of hatred came into my heart for her. Love is the best thing, yes, but until things go wrong. Once things go off track, love hurts, tortures and makes you cry. Just like love is the best feeling, the pain that comes with it is the worst. Who would know this better than me? It's as if the world around starts falling upon you. So much so that your dreams, emotions, feelings, everything shatters irreparably.

I didn't realise when my thoughts dissolved into nothingness and I faded into melancholy.

The next day, I woke up around noon. I had a splitting headache and still felt dizzy and sleepy. I opened my eyes slightly, looked around and slept again. When I woke up again, it was six in the evening. I woke up perhaps because I was hungry. I found myself sleeping diagonally. It was a dark room with the stench of wine everywhere. I had experienced such a situation only with friends in college, when a group of boys smoked pot the whole night and I had gone to meet them. Their room used to be filled with friends and smoke. I detested such situations, but now when I looked all around me, my eyes filled with tears again.

I peeped out of the bed-corner and picked up the pillow that had been kicked off. A few minutes later, I gathered myself up, took the towel and dragged myself to the shower. I stood under the water jet for several minutes, as if trying to wash off the memories of Ashima with the water into the gutter.

I dried myself up and put the same t-shirt that I had worn the previous day. I was feeling hungry, so I ordered a pizza.

I checked my mobile and saw ten missed calls and twenty WhatsApp messages. I ignored them all.

I looked around my dingy flat; it looked like it was going to drag me into the deep hole of loneliness and depression. My inner voice coaxed me to change and start walking on the path that leads to happiness. Stuck between the battle of the mind and the heart, I promised myself that I was going to do something about it. Although I had made such promises in the past also, tomorrow had never come. This time, it had to change.

I was in class eight when the feeling of unrequited love first hit me. Or maybe I finally began to understand what was wrong with my understanding of love. Like most boys my age, I craved for my mother's attention and appreciation. And all I got was my father taking me out to the market on days that my mother scolded me. He offered to buy me new kind of sweets and chocolates that I loved, but how could that have compensated for love! When these things went on and on, I realized that although I didn't hate her for this incapability, she was clearly devoid of love.

As a child, what I loved the most was being in my own shell. I loved the world of my imagination, where I was the hero. Having grown up in a place where there wasn't much scope for romantic or quixotic explorations, I had to create my own utopias and shangrilas.

Not much changed even as I grew up. I remained an introvert, fearful of rejection. I mean, imagine! If your own mother thought you to be useless, what could you have expected from the world! Crowds made me anxious and my insecurity and fear scaled new heights at the thought of maintaining multiple relationships. That's why I always believed in having a few, yet strong relationships.

Books became my companions in those days. I realized that the vast world of books could open that door for me through which I could not only re-create and imagine, but also explore the worlds created by others.

The feeling of unrequited love was so ingrained in my heart that I believed in one thing that was once said by Rumi: "Choose Love, love! Without the sweet life of Love, living is a burden – as you have seen." For some inexplicable reasons, I always believed that the 'you' that Rumi referred to was me. As I had seen life as a burden, a heaviness on the heart every second.

She was standing there with another guy. But why like that? So close?

"Hey," I said.

Ashima was startled as she had been too engrossed with the new guy. "Sanjeev! What the fuck are you doing here?"

"I just wanted to talk to my girlfriend. It has been quite a long time since we talked. I called you so many times, but neither did you pick up the phone, nor did you call back."

"Sanjeev, you need to go. I don't want to talk right now." The other guy was silent. She turned towards him, but before she could say anything to him, I almost shouted, "Why?" What's the problem?"

"Because I don't want to," she replied sternly. The anger within me started boiling.

"And why is that? Because you are too happy with this new guy?"

"Yes, he is good enough for me to be happy about. Happy? Now just get lost. I don't want to talk to you or see your face. Whatever there was between us, just forget it. It was just a lie."

I wondered if she was possessed. She was hurting me more and more. "How could you say that? You're telling me that the entire year that we were together was just a lie!"

"Listen carefully Sanjeev, because I won't say it again. You don't seem to be fine. You need to move on."

"What is that even supposed to mean? I was perfectly fine when you felt I was cute. I was more than fine when you loved me and changed my life. Because of you, I started understanding what love can mean to someone. Didn't I tell you that my relationship with you was the source of my joy, that you were someone with whom I can spend the rest of my life? How can all this be a lie?" *I said stonewalling my tears.*

"What relationship you are talking about, Sanjeev? I was infatuated with you and that died down with time. Life with you was nothing less than hell. You were so possessive; you didn't give any breathing space to me. How could you even think that I could live by talking only to you? It's not my problem that you didn't have a friend to hang out with or talk to. Maybe that's why you don't have any friends. Because you are just a mad and insane guy who can let nobody be happy. Trust me, not a single girl would want to be with you. You have nothing to talk about except your emotional problems with your mother. You are so needy all the time, you could might as well go and beg for love. I wonder how someone can have such a loser kind of attitude with zero self-esteem! What can you boast of anyway? A stupid engineering degree from a shitty college. Who would want to be with such a guy who has no future and a mind full of need? This was our fucking relationship, Mister Sanjeev."

I was aghast, totally numb with her words. But she wasn't done yet. "Did you ever get me a gift? Did you ever kiss me? Not even when I literally begged you to. With you, I didn't know what feelings one has in love…what it is to celebrate Valentine's Day with a lover.

And what did you do on my birthday except arguing with me over why was I more willing to party with my other friends rather than you?" She stopped, heaved a deep sigh with her eyes tightly shut. *"Now, if you have any bit of self-respect left, just leave and don't ever call me again."*

My eyes were wide open with shock. I didn't know what to say. I was left wondering why she had never discussed it with me earlier. I could have changed things and made her stay. I could only murmur, "You are my girlfriend. You can't leave me like this. I love you a lot. You are the centre of my existence…" and before I could finish my sentence, the mute spectator interrupted, "Listen, mister. Enough of this shit. She was *your girlfriend. Now she is* mine. *So just get lost."*

I looked at Ashima. But she ignored me and left me with no other option but to accept what had just happened. His words were like arrows that pierced my heart; but her silence was like death itself.

❀

It had been several years, but the whole situation was still fresh in my mind. Like it had happened yesterday. Despite all that had happened, and no matter how much things had changed, the memories of her remained the same. There was still a soft corner for her in my heart.

Today again, the entire conversation crossed my mind. I thought for a moment and decided to call Gaurav.

Before making this call, I had also contemplated calling Rishabh. But I had just had a tiff with him and I wasn't sure if he would lend me a ear right now. Not for my pain, at least. Having no other option for tonight, I decided to give Gaurav a call.

I had connected with Gaurav on Facebook. He had sent me a friend request after reading my book. And like every other friend request, I had accepted his too. Within a few minutes of acceptance, a message had popped up. It started with 'Hi', but soon the conversation steered towards my book. He told me straight away, "I read your book and even read a few bloggers' reviews. I kind of liked it and appreciate your effort."

I said thanks and continued to talk about other aspects of the book. I liked the conversation with him. At the end of the conversation, he requested me to read a short story that he had written. Till now, I had thought of him to be just a reader. I was usually bombarded with friend requests from readers. It surprised me when he requested me to read his work. Out of courtesy, I told him to mail it to me and gave him my email id before closing the chat window.

One day when I had nothing to do, I thought of reading Gaurav's story. After reading the first few lines, I was agape as it was one of the finest pieces of writing I had ever read. So without reading any further, I logged in to Facebook and checked his profile. He was a doctor from Assam and wrote short stories as a passion. He was elder to me, of course much more intelligent too. I pinged him and asked him about his writing. From that day till now, we had been discussing everything under the sun and had become very good friends. He also told me that he had learnt creative writing from England and that's why his language was influenced by British English.

I knew that it being Sunday, he would be out with his friends in a pub or somewhere hep, but I still thought of giving it a try. After four rings, he picked up the call. I could see that the call timer had started, but I couldn't hear a word. There was a lot of noise in the background. After a few seconds, he came out of the pub to talk to me.

"Hi Sanjeev! Is everything okay? Is there anything urgent because I am hanging out with my friends," he said.

"Yes, I wanted to talk about those dreams that I once told you about."

"Yes, I remember. Did something happen again?"

"It's getting worse day by day, and my mind and sleep aren't peaceful at all. Memories are haunting me again," I said and started sobbing.

He heard me out but went quiet. I wondered if he was there at all. I overheard him saying in the background, "Siddharth, I need to go. You guys carry on, I will catch you in a while."

"Yes, Sanjeev. Please continue," he said, resuming the call.

I told him about my sleeplessness and even about the wine that I had to drink to catch a wink of sleep. He listened to me attentively and then said, "See, the major issue with you is the loneliness. You neither meet people, nor interact with the people who meet you. It has been several months that you visited any new places as well. You really need to go out. Dreams come to your mind because memories occupy your subconscious mind. You really need to change the thoughts in your subconscious mind. Your subconscious mind is everything. It records everything – the way you think, behave and do your activities. So until you change the way you think, your thoughts won't change and it would keep coming to you in the form of dreams. Plus, Sanjeev, the past is past. People have moved on. You must realize that the future is way more important for you. It's your life and you are the true master of your happiness. You made the mistake of giving the key to your happiness to someone else, and see where you have landed yourself. You have to take control of your life and let the past go."

"I tried, Gaurav. I tried to throw it all out of me through that diary."

"I know Sanjeev. But sometimes that's not enough. You really need to come out of your room and start meeting new people. Maybe someone like you, who thinks and acts like you. You must go out and meet like-minded people."

"I will try, Gaurav. But it's easier said than done. How will I find new people?"

"At least try. There's no harm in trying. As far as sleep is concerned, I will prescribe some sleeping pills. You go and get them. It's quite mild and it won't harm you. I will just message you the name of the tablet."

I said okay and then hung up. When I received Gaurav's message, I called the boy who was the caretaker of the flat. I wrote down the name of the tablet on a piece of paper and asked him to bring it to me. I sat in silence, pondering over what Gaurav had just said. I knew I needed to change, but I didn't know where to begin.

The caretaker came back empty-handed; the pharmacist had refused to give the medicine without a proper prescription. He returned the piece of paper and the money I had given him. Before he closed the door, he asked in an innocent tone, "The shopkeeper told me these are sleeping pills. Is there any problem you want to talk about?" His eyes implored mine.

I said, "Nothing. Everything is fine." And he closed the door behind him.

I called up Gaurav to ask for his suggestion. His phone was busy, so I waited for him to call me up. It was around 9 p.m. when he called back.

"Yea, tell me Sanjeev," he asked." I just saw your missed call."

"Nothing serious. Just that the chemist refused to give the medicine you had suggested. What now?"

"Oh. Is it? It's not an over the counter drug. It needs a prescription. What I can do at this moment is to courier you the medicines, but let me warn you that this is just a temporary solution. You really need to force yourself and gather your will to come out of this state of mind."

I agreed with him. Few moments later, he said, "Sometimes what we make for ourselves in years shatters in seconds; what we are left with is a debris of memories, dreams and emotions. It's quite tough to forget it. These things recede slowly, and that too when you keep yourself busy. Memories work this way only. Why don't you join some club or classes to learn something that you always wanted to learn? This way you will meet some like-minded people as well and you will be alone in your room on weekends. Life is too short to feel sorry for yourself. Stop thinking about it. I know it's easy for me to say, but I would wish for you to enjoy life. You don't know your future... so make a difference, man."

I had known all along what he had just told me. The whole point was its implementation. He had given me a good idea to make the change possible. "It's quite a good idea. I will think about it."

"Yes! And don't worry, you will find your true soulmate someday," he said in an assuring tone.

"Soulmate? Do you really believe in this fairy tale concept?" I said in a surprised tone as it piqued my interest.

"Of course. You know the story, right? Of the soulmates?"

"I don't think so," I said confused.

"Okay, let me narrate it to you."

"I am all ears." I have always enjoyed such stories and had a keen interest in reading, but to believe such stories was completely out of the question for me.

"Well, long back, humans had four arms, four legs and a single head made of two faces. And there were three genders: man, woman and the androgynous. The former with two sets of genitalia each, with the androgynous having both male and female genitalia. The men were children of the sun, the women were children of the earth, and the androgynous were the children of the moon, which was born of the sun and earth. It is said that humans had great strength at the time and threatened to conquer the gods. The gods were then faced with the prospect of destroying the humans with lightning as they had done with the Titans, but then they would lose out on the tributes given to the gods by humans. Zeus developed a creative solution by splitting humans in half as punishment for humanity's pride and doubling the number of humans who would give tribute to the gods. These split humans were in utter misery to the point where they would not eat and would perish. So Apollo had sewn them up and reconstituted their bodies with the navel being the only remnant harkening back to their original form. Each human would then only have one set of genitalia and would forever long for his/her other half; the other half of his/her soul."

"Interesting. But how would one realize if the other is the soulmate?" I asked.

"It is said that when the two find each other, there is an unspoken understanding, they feel unified and would lie with each other in unity and would know no greater joy than that."

"Great. I hope I meet someone like this soon," I joked.

"You will and for that, you have to go outside and meet new people."

"Alright. If for nothing else, then for this story, I will give it a shot."

❀

After dinner, I sat down and started thinking about Gaurav's suggestion. I was ready to go out and involve myself in something. But what?

When nothing came to my mind for quite a long time, I made a list and started pondering over each one. It began with:

Dance-Salsa – No

Guitar – No. I had learnt guitar for a month and didn't like it much.

I was getting confused, but when my eyes roved to the DSLR I had bought for myself a year ago, my eyes shone and spoke with joy, "Yes, photography!"

It was around 2 a.m. and I wasn't sleepy at all. I was happy that the dreams were not going to haunt me today, because I was wide awake. With nothing else to do, I started researching about photography classes for beginners in Delhi. After researching for an hour, I noted down a few contact details to call the next day to enquire more about the courses from the office.

"Joining these classes may help me forget her," I said to myself and picked up a book to read. After reading a few pages, my mind started thinking about the theory of soulmates that Gaurav had narrated a few hours back.

"Is it really true? Will I find my soulmate too?" These questions crossed my mind.

There was a hope... but it was dim and not anywhere in sight yet.

The next day was Monday – usually a cruel day for most office goers. But I reached office around 8:15 a.m. and directly went to the canteen to have breakfast. The only people I could see were the cleaning staff. One of them said, "Good morning, sir."

I reciprocated with a nod and a smile, and took my seat. I wanted to finalize my admission to the photography classes and had to at least finish with my research. I quickly had breakfast and ran back to my desk, switching on the laptop with a swift push to the power button. My life also seemed to have been switched on suddenly. I was so engrossed in my laptop, looking up for courses and checking what they comprised, that I didn't realize when the clock struck nine. My colleagues had started coming in; some must have said hello but I had absolutely no memory of it. I was finally interrupted by Vineet, whose seat was right next to mine. He patted me on my shoulder when I was engrossed switching between many tabs. I looked up and saw him grinning like he had caught me watching porn.

"What are you doing?" he asked.

"Nothing much. Just checking out some photography courses," I said.

"Oh, are you planning to join one?" he said, keeping his bag on his seat.

"Considering it. You tell me, how was your weekend?"

"It was great. We all went to the pub on Saturday night. Abhinav tried to hit on the girls there, like he keeps doing here as well, but like all other times, no success." We both shared a light laugh. Abhinav was notoriously infamous among all the office girls too, though he did all that light-heartedly.

Vineet continued, "I even tried calling you. You didn't pick up the call. Where were you?"

"Oh, did you? I am sorry I didn't realize I had missed your call."

"Dude, we had some good fun. You should have been there."

"Next time, definitely," I said, looking at my laptop. Then with a sudden realization, I asked him, "Did you see how much work this new manager has given us?"

"Yes, fucking bastard. Can you believe he called me last evening and asked me to prepare a report last night itself while he was busy fucking whores?" His tone suddenly changed.

"What? But I thought he is married." I looked at him curiously.

"Do you seriously think he cares about that? The way he talks to his subordinates, especially hot chicks, tells us otherwise." He was fuming. I wondered if the manager had tried to flirt with his girlfriend too, who was in the same office, though on another project.

"Did you send the report?"

"I did, but half-baked. I am sure he will be spitting fire today. Let's see."

Vineet and Abhinav had joined the office a day before me, and I ended up spending a majority of my time with them. Out of habit, Vineet kept abusing the manager, and as if knowing he would, the manager continued torturing him. Since it was a start-up, most of the employees were quite young. Few experienced employees were higher level executives. The new manager had joined a few weeks back, but he had a habit of micro-managing us. I must have been born under some lucky star, for he wasn't the manager I was supposed to report to, though I did handle his work sometimes. And those few times, he had made me sit in the office for longer.

What irked me the most about him was that he never came to the office on time himself, but if we got delayed by even a few minutes, he forced us to apply for leave. It was downright cruel most times. Thankfully his seat was on the floor above ours, so he could not snoop in on us more than once or twice a day. Vineet told us during lunch time once that the manager had purposefully chosen to sit on the floor above. There were fewer employees on that floor and he had his desk bang opposite Mahima's. He was reported to ogle at her more than look into his tasks each day. Someone had overheard that he was planning to give her the best rating in the next appraisal.

His mood calmed after sharing his woes with me, and we both got to work. Around eleven, most people left for the tea break and I could see a very few people around. I called up the numbers I had taken down, to enquire about the photography classes and fee. I didn't want many to know about this, otherwise I would have ended up just answering their questions rather than making those calls.

"Hello, A to Z Photography Institute. How may I help you?" A sweet voice asked.

"Hi, this is Sanjeev here. I wanted to know about your short-term courses and the fees for it."

"Sure sir. Can I please know what kind of course you'd be interested in?" she asked politely.

"I was checking your website but haven't been able to gather much. Can you please brief me a bit?"

"Definitely sir. There are two kinds of courses in the short-term category: weekday classes and weekend classes. The weekend classes would cost you slightly more though, because they are very popular and we have limited seats. Let me send you all the details in an email. In case of any confusion or query, you can give us a call back. We would be happy to help you." I hurriedly disconnected the phone, without even hearing her out. I had seen the manager walking towards my desk. But to my relief, he passed onto the other side.

I decided to wait till the manager was gone and then continue with this R&D. I walked towards Abhinav's desk at the far end as soon as it was time for lunch – exactly 1 p.m. It was kind of obvious that we would go for lunch exactly at 1 for two reasons: first, we get hot food in the canteen; second, we could easily get a clean table.

Vineet was not at his desk, so I assumed he would come directly to the canteen. It was our unsaid code. Abhinav was already in the canteen occupying the same table on which I had sat on the very first day. He was as usual involved with his phone, either swiping left or right on Tinder, or checking out beautiful girls on Instagram, gasping in between.

I sat across him and asked, "Where is Vineet?"

"How would I know? He always comes with you."

"He does, but he wasn't at his seat."

"Must be with the manager. Regarding last night's report."

"Okay, let me bring my lunch. I am starving." It took me five minutes to order lunch and I came back to the table with a big plate. He was still engrossed in his phone.

"Fuck man!"

"What happened?" I stopped eating, the spoonful of rice hanging in mid-air.

"See these girls. So many of our office girls are on Tinder. And when you talk to them, they behave as if I am some weird alien trying to socialize. Like I will pounce on them."

"What's the big deal if they are on Tinder?" I asked, finally taking the rice to its rightful destination.

"Because when you talk to them, or ask them out for a cup of coffee, they just say they have boyfriends. Then what the fuck are they on Tinder for?"

"Because of idiot and dumb people like you, you know, who just keep explaining logics and theories on the lunch table. Will you just go, talk and fuck her?" A raging tone came from behind my back. I turned back to see a fuming Vineet.

"Seems you had a lovely meeting with the manager," Abhinav said sarcastically.

"If I was allowed to kill any one person, I would kill this bastard," Vineet spat.

"Calm down," said Abhinav. "Look at this girl." He turned his phone screen towards him. "Do you recognize her?"

"No, and if you ask again, I will throw your new phone into this glass of water. Nothing else to do? Keep checking out girls on Tinder and Instagram." Hearing that, Abhinav quickly pulled his phone back.

"What happened?" I asked finally.

"The same story. Last night's report. He pointed out so many mistakes and said that I am not paying attention to work these days. How the fuck can one prepare a report on Sunday night? And that too being drunk. When I said this, he didn't even listen to me."

Abhinav did not pay attention to Vineet' rambling, as usual. He continued, "Above all, he was saying that this kind of shitty work will reflect in my appraisal. Bloody fucker, he always threatens me with this appraisal bit. And he will give that Mahima the best rating."

"He is like that, Vineet. Not the first time. Calm down. Don't take it personally."

He became quiet when Mahima came and sat down next to Abhinav.

"Hi guys. What's up?"

"Hey, Mahima." It was the Abhinav who spoke first. Before that, he hadn't even bothered to look at us. "Vineet was talking about you only."

Vineet frowned at him. "Really Vineet?" she looked at Vineet and asked. I looked at Vineet too, waiting to hear what he was going to say.

"Nothing much. We were talking about appraisals. And I am sure you are going to get a five-star rating. You work so hard," he said in a slow tone.

"Hope so," she said.

I looked at Abhinav. He was laughing meekly.

For the next couple of days, I couldn't visit the photography institute as the work load was a bit heavy. The same girl that I had once called to get information had called me twice in these four days, asking when I would be planning to give them a visit. I just assured her that I would soon.

I came out of office a bit earlier than usual on Friday and directly reached the photography institute. A girl at the reception welcomed me and asked me to wait in the waiting room. Sometime later, some other girl came and discussed the brochure.

"Sir, as you have been told, we have two programs. Weekdays and weekend classes. In the former, three classes will be conducted on Monday, Wednesday and Friday, respectively. The latter consists of classes on Saturday and Sunday. On Sundays, there will be field trip photography after the class."

After considering all the options, I opted for the weekday classes. I filled up the form and paid the fee. I had to start the class the coming Monday, two days later.

The next day, I was enjoying my day off when I received the courier that Gaurav had sent me. I knew it had the same sleeping pills that I had been in desperate need of till a few days back. But I decided not to take them. The greatest tragedy of human life is when your heart longs for love and there is no one around to love you. Deep inside me, I longed for love, not for these pills.

I stared at the packet for a few minutes and finally, threw the pills in the dustbin. Gaurav's idea was worth more than the pills. This passion for photography and meeting new people had infused in me a newfound hope.

For the first photography class, I walked in ten minutes before the scheduled time. That had been my habit ever since school. I was escorted to an empty classroom at the end of the corridor. The room was well-lit and the chairs were arranged rather thoughtfully, with enough space around each chair. There was a small podium towards which the chairs were facing, behind which was a white board. There was also a small table next to the podium. I looked around the room to find the right spot where I didn't remain in the spotlight and could also have the best view. After certain useless mental calculations, I chose a seat in the third row, somewhere in the middle. I felt weird being in a classroom again. I had been sure that there would be no more classes post engineering, which had been four years of jail for me. I was feeling twitchy, but strangely exhilarated as I was here for something that I had wanted to learn for so long.

Within the next ten minutes, five or six students came and occupied the chairs starting from the second row. The first row was still empty, and seeing this, a faint smile appeared on my lips. It reminded me of my college days where students always started filling up the chairs beginning from the last rows. When it seemed no more people were going to come, as most of the seats were taken, I counted a total of fifteen students, out of which five were girls. Most of the boys were checking out the girls in the class, while the girls were not paying much attention to them.

It reminded me of my conversation with Abhinav and Vineet over lunch the same day. I had mentioned to them that I would be starting my photography classes.

Vineet remarked, "See, Abhinav. Sanjeev has joined some real place where he will meet hot chicks. You know how you get girls?"

"How?" asked Abhinav.

"You can't just go to a bar and ask a girl 'Can I buy you a drink?' It only happens in Hollywood or Bollywood. So, it would be better for you to start thinking practically and stop wasting your time on Instagram or Tinder. It's all useless." Vineet laughed.

"Oh, please. I know I will get girls soon. And my way is the best way."

"Yes, in your dreams." And Vineet started laughing out loud.

"I will also be joining tango classes, yoga classes and guitar classes," Abhinav said in a voice radiant with hope.

"Yoga classes?" Vineet's eyes dilated with surprise. "Okay, even if you find some girls there, how are you going to approach them? Excuse me! You have nice yoga pants. Will you let me inside it?" He mimicked Abhinav and chuckled.

"Enough!" Abhinav was heartbroken. "I will show you when I will have the hottest girlfriend."

I assumed some boys would have joined photography classes with the same hope. Eye candy. A faint smile crossed my lips. A creak of the door broke my reverie and all heads turned towards it. A middle-aged man entered with a camera, and many lenses, ranging from small ones to a huge lens. He also had a few DVDs in his hand. He walked towards the podium and smiled at all of us. It was obvious that he was the one to take us through the course, and he confirmed it with the introduction. His name was Ramesh. He had quite a pleasant face with short hair.

"What better and more appropriate way to start off the classes than by mentioning one of the most famous and influential photographer's words – *Your first ten thousand photographs are your worst*, said Henri Cartier-Bresson."

There was a round of light laughter after which he continued, "Hello everyone. I am glad to see you all here and hope to have some great times with you. We will start with the basics and proceed towards other aspects of photography with time. But let me tell you something, photography is more about practical experience than just sitting in a class and hearing someone talk. So, after every fifteen or twenty odd minutes of basic guidelines, we will see how it works practically."

He looked at us, smiling enthusiastically. Then suddenly his smile became wider as he said, "But before we start, why don't you guys come and fill this first row? I am sure this won't be boring. And moreover, when I will demonstrate on the camera, it would be difficult for those in the last rows to see."

He was looking at me when he finished his sentence. I understood the unsaid direction. So, I stood up, collected all my gear and shifted to the first row. In between, some guy asked a question and Ramesh got involved with him.

A noise from across the room interrupted everyone. The door opened and bam – someone had her hands full with a camera box, a camera bag, a manual and every other thing that tumbled onto the floor one after the other. The manual had slid towards my foot.

"Easy, easy. Hope the camera is fine." Ramesh walked towards her, helping her gather everything. I couldn't see her face as she had bent down to pick her stuff, and Ramesh was covering some space too.

I picked up the manual and looked up. The entire room was looking at her. It would have been quite humiliating for her if it would have been college or school. I knew this feeling better than anyone. Like the time when I had to give a class lecture during engineering. Out of fear, I just blabbered about the topic and finished it as quickly as I could. It was followed by a huge round of laughter from every corner of the room, including the teacher who laughed sitting on the last bench; or the time when I ran from the stage during Independence Day speech seeing so many people sitting and looking at me.

And because I had felt humiliated on several occasions in the past and I wanted to save her from the same fate, I knocked down my empty camera box onto the floor. All eyes shifted to me then. I bent to pick up the box and looked at her; her eyes met mine. Her hands were now full of everything related to a camera. She smiled and walked towards me. I quickly picked up the box and kept it on a chair. I settled easily, like nothing had happened, quite subtly. She came and sat right next to me.

I looked at her and smiled. To my surprise, she was looking at me with her big eyes and an even bigger grin. I looked at her closely. She was plump, with a round heavy face, long hair falling at the back of her nape. She appeared extremely cute to me. She seemed that kind of girl who we see in movies as the hero or heroine's best friend, who would be extremely nice, clear-hearted and easy to be friends with; who nobody wanted to be engaged with romantically.

She kept smiling at me. And although I had been a tad uneasy in the beginning, I kind of liked it now.

Ramesh started showing some photographs on the projector and started explaining the technicalities. At which combination of shutter speed, aperture and ISO were the pictures clicked. I was mesmerized to see the quality of the photographs. At the end of the classes, Ramesh asked each one of us what kind of photography we wanted to do. I said portraits and landscapes, although wild life photography also fascinated me.

He went towards the back benchers and a sweet voice greeted me from one side.

"Hi, I am Ruchita," the girl sitting beside me said.

I looked at her. She smiled and continued, "Thanks for saving me from the embarrassment."

"It's my pleasure," I said and started reading the terms written on the slides.

"I thought you'd tell me your name."

"Oh, sorry. I am Sanjeev Ranjan."

"Nice meeting you, Sanjeev." She smiled with a twinkle in her eyes.

Ramesh, in the meantime, came towards the podium. He said, "It's great to see excitement mainly for portraits and landscapes. We will focus more on that then. Even during field trips, we will focus on these two. Before we go into any other technicality of the camera setting and understand which combination we shall use during photography, we must learn how to handle a camera. With even a little shaking, the photos can get blurred. So, everyone take your camera and follow me."

He picked up his camera and all of us followed suit, while he continued, "First of all, we are going to use both hands to handle the camera. There is a groove just beside the click button, from there you all will take the camera in one hand. Also wrap up the strap in your hand, as it would help you in case the camera slips out of your grip. Then use your other hand to rest beneath the lens part to give it support."

I tried to follow him but since I was left-handed, it was the opposite for me. If I kept the camera in my left hand, then I won't be able to press the click key that was on the right side; and if I held the camera in my right hand, then there would be a possibility that the camera would shake just before I pressed the click key. Out of no options, I held the camera in my left hand and clicked a photograph using the right hand. As expected, it came out blurred.

"Let me help you." It was her again. When she saw me getting confused with the camera, she offered her help.

"Yeah, thanks. I am a leftie and this is complicated for me." I smiled sheepishly.

"I saw that. But you can still click pictures the usual way. Just make your hand steady and place the camera steadily on your left palm. Initially, you can lock the lens from manual to auto-focus. It will help you get the focus easily." I followed her and clicked a picture of her.

She looked at the screen and said, "See, this is better. Less blurred than the previous ones."

It was indeed better than the previous photograph.

"Thanks. Have you done this before?" I asked her, curious to know how she knew this much.

"Yes, kind of. During college fests and family functions. I know nothing apart from this. I just click photographs in auto mode always." She said and laughed.

And that was how I met Ruchita. I had never realized that this small conversation would become a precious part of my life in times to come. And also that something beautiful would begin.

But when we met for the next class, her madness brought out different colours.

Even though I had barely attended one class of the photography lessons, it had made me hopeful for a brighter future. I felt less stressed. That night, I slept peacefully after a long time after reading up on photography on various online portals. My mind had found a new topic to pursue and I was loving it.

I was eagerly waiting for the next class, but office was competing neck to neck with my newfound passion; there was a lot of work these days.

The next day, I was out for tea at a tea point right outside the office building. The tea this old man made was a welcome change from the tea made by the office machine. Vineet called up just when I was about to take the first sip of my tea.

He sounded irritated when he asked, "Where are you?"

"Out for tea. You were not at your desk, so I came alone. What happened?"

"Don't ask! You wait there. I really need a smoke."

He joined me soon after, and he sure looked angry.

"What happened to you now?" I asked.

"Nothing yaar. Same old shit. I am tired of this same useless crap every day. You know what happened? I saw Mahima with my manager last night at the pub."

Vineet had been burning his blood over Mahima and the manager, but this story never interested me much. So I just nodded and said, "That's the usual shit then. What's so shocking about that?"

"Exactly, it's so usual now that people have stopped paying attention. Anyway, I just mentioned it." He ordered tea for himself and asked, "Where is our Insta guy?"

"Must be busy ogling at someone somewhere." He shook his head as a crooked smile appeared on his face. I had just finished my sentence when I saw him coming from the other side.

"What happened? Why are you laughing?" Vineet asked irritably, seeing Abhinav grinning like he had just won the lottery. I knew an interesting conversation was about to unfold, so I decided to just enjoy as a spectator without interrupting them.

"I just got to know the secret to impress girls," he said with pride in his voice.

"Oh really? So you finally joined salsa or tango classes?"

"Not yet. But I will do that soon too. But for now, I have figured that you need to be less needy and desperate for a girl to attract and impress one. Then only they will talk to you and date you."

"What crap do you keep thinking? And from where did you get this theory anyway? Did someone finally tell you on Instagram or Tinder that you look like a desperate guy?"

"No! I am much sought after on social media, dude. People love me, especially girls. I think they are hesitant to approach me, that's all. But all that aside, let me tell you more about the idea." Then he smiled mysteriously and asked, "You know this guy, Vikrant?"

"Who, that quality section guy?"

"Yes, the same. So what happened is this. He sits on my floor and had been trying to talk to Aakriti for so very long. Most of us have seen him asking her out during lunch or tea or just pretending to pass by and say hello. But most of the time, she refused. He tried to crack jokes, which were never as good as mine, mind you! In short, he would make a fool out of himself just for her company for lunch."

"So what's the point? He didn't ask her and she went with him today?"

"No, you loser! I wonder if there will ever be a day when you'll think good for your bhai!" he said pointing at himself. We both chuckled, as he continued, "The point is that Aakriti had tried to talk to me many times, and I never paid attention to her." At this, Vineet and I started laughing, making fun of Abhinav.

He seemed unruffled, and smiled. "Last Friday, when she came to me for some work, I acted like I didn't care." That was the last straw and Vineet and I burst into a loud laugh.

Vineet managed to stop and say, "*Abey jhuthe*! You drool over girls who don't give you any *bhao*. If a girl as much as even bats an eyelid at you, you'd think she is head over heels in love with you. You think we will believe this shit about you and Aakriti?"

"We went out yesterday. We had dinner," he said with the pride of a king who had just won a battle.

"What the fuck man? I don't believe you." Vineet was sure this was all made up.

"I knew you guys won't believe me. That's why I asked for a selfie." He showed me his phone. It was true. He had clicked a selfie with Aakriti at some fancy place.

Vineet snatched the phone from his hand and gave it a closer look. The laughter changed to a smile and Vineet patted on his shoulder, saying, "Great! That's why you were not picking up the phone last evening."

"Of course. And I had lunch with her today."

We thought Abhinav's efforts had finally paid off. Even if not an affair, he had managed a couple of meals.

We headed back to the office after finishing our tea. After a few more hours of grueling work, I left for the photography class which I really looked forward to.

It had been an informative class that evening; I felt a whole lot of technical jargon had been thrown at us, but the excitement was brimming. The instructor started wrapping his gear at the end of the class. "See you all next week," he said jovially, but stopped abruptly as if he had remembered something suddenly.

"Since it's the weekend, don't forget to practice. Go crazy, click anything you see beauty in. We will all share our experiences in the Monday class. And if some of you are interested, a group of photographers will be at the Humayun's Tomb this Sunday. I will also be there for some time. You're all most welcome to join us."

The murmurs in the class indicated that there was some planning and excitement about the proposed plan. Everyone started leaving the classroom one by one.

Ruchita nudged me while I was packing up my gear. I looked up at her and raised my eyebrows.

"Have you got some time?" she asked.

"Now?"

"Yes."

"Yeah, I am almost free. Nothing much to do at this hour," I said casually.

"Cool! Let's have some fun then. My parents are out for some party and won't be back till midnight. We have a good two hours."

"That's good. But what are we going to do at this hour? Plus, we have all this gear with us which is tough to carry and roam about," I asked, walking out of the building with her.

She didn't reply for a few moments, so I looked at her. I noticed that her gaze was stuck on something. I followed her eyes and saw a *golgappa* stall on the opposite side of the road.

"Do you like golgappas?" she asked, still not moving her eyes.

"Yup."

"Then let's have a competition of eating the most golgappas!" she said with a twinkle in her eyes. "Are you ready?"

Without waiting for an answer, she started walking towards the stall and I had to increase my pace to catch up with her

"This is fine, but I thought you wanted to have fun?" I said, confused at what this girl was up to.

She stopped short, turned around and pulled my cheeks, saying, "Oh, my boy! Everything is fun if you start enjoying it. Now, be ready to lose this battle."

"Yeah? Only time will tell who loses and who wins," I also said excitedly. "Wait, but what does one get if the other loses?" Now it was my turn to be mischievous.

"You should think what you are going to get for me, because you are surely going to lose," she said proudly.

I laughed mocking her over confidence as we both reached the stall.

Out of sheer excitement, I said, "Bhaiya, let's begin! Start firing your best shots. Gladiator is ready."

The guy handing out the golgappas to a couple of teenagers looked at me as if I had spoken some foreign language. He looked paler than his frail body could hide. Ruchita started laughing when I uttered the word 'Gladiator'.

I realized what I had done. And smiling to myself more than Ruchita, I said, "Okay, fine! No need to laugh. You called it a battle to begin with. Focus on the counts, madam. You're on the verge of losing even before we begin."

The stall guy had already given us the plates in the meantime; the game was on!

"How many golgappas sir?"

"Till she begs me to stop." I began laughing and the man stared at us again. "Bhaiya, I will tell you when to stop. You keep counting till then." I winked at her.

Initially, I kept a count of how many we had eaten, but in the next several minutes, none of us raised our hand. Nor did we ask him to stop. But I had lost count by now. After every piece of golgappa, she used to look at me and give me a wink like I wouldn't be able to eat more and would indicate to stop. But that wasn't to be.

A couple of minutes later, Ruchita's eyes looked red and it appeared that not another golgappa would go into her mouth without torturing her. I could have easily beaten her because I still had a lot of capacity. I could see her struggling, literally shoving the balls of spicy water into her mouth. A sudden thought crept up and told me – every time in life that I have wished to win, I have lost. Today, I wanted to lose this battle for a girl who had made me happy and made attempts to remove boredom from my life.

I smiled at her, and saw that she had one golgappa in her mouth, one in her hand ready to be pushed in and another one in her plate. She had slowed down for sure. Even though my plate was empty and the golgappa guy asked me to bring the plate closer so he could put another one, I said, "No, I am done."

I threw the plate into the dustbin nearby and turned to look at her. She looked relieved and her face had a winning shine. She wanted to shout, but couldn't. Her lips were ready to open and throw out the golgappa still in her mouth.

I smiled and asked her to relax. "Finish eating first. I know you have won; you can taunt me later."

She had won the competition by a margin of one golgappa. Even though I had lost, though deliberately, I felt happiness within me. It was true that you don't need to win every single battle or argument with your friends or someone you love.

I paid the bill for the golgappas, because I had lost.

"So? Got beaten by a lady Gladiator today?" she teased.

"No, never! Gladiator's stomach turned traitor today. To your luck!" I said.

"Huh, losers always have such lame excuses. Nobody can beat me in a golgappa competition."

"Alright madam. I shall remember that." She smiled victoriously, and I asked, "Now where are we going?"

"To the mall," she said. "Window shopping perhaps."

"Okay. The tiffin boy is also not going to come today. So we will eat at the food court before we leave. What say?"

She looked at me suspiciously. "You have just had a whole lot of golgappas, and you had no space to have more. And now you're suddenly hungry?"

Shit, I thought, I was such a fool. I covered up saying, "I didn't mean eating right away. After an hour, I am sure even you will be hungry."

I had tried to cover up, but her naughty smile meant she had caught me. Or maybe not.

Within these two weeks that we had spent together at the class and outside it, I had understood that Ruchita was quite an extrovert, a typical Punjabi girl. Flamboyant. She barely cared for what others thought of her and was free-spirited. She made friends easily, but didn't approach many people. She wanted to keep every friend happy, so perhaps controlled the number wisely. She was slightly plump, but the way she carried herself made her look very attractive. She was always cheerful; the first instance of that was shown on the very first day when all her gear had fallen, and she had still got up laughing with the others. The way she pulled me towards the food stalls after some classes assured me that she was a foodie at heart.

We took an auto rickshaw to the mall and reached within a few minutes. We could have walked but Ruchita had insisted on saving time. She did some window shopping and took me to a Vero Moda outlet.

"I am not going in. It's for girls only. It will be awkward for me," I protested and stopped in front of the store.

"Come on! There's nothing like that. They sell clothes for girls only, yes, but they don't throw men out. See, there are already many boys inside," she said, pointing at the store and the people inside.

I looked inside and shouted at her, "Yes! Because they are the salespersons, you duffer."

"Oh, then look at that guy! Spiked hair, you see? Must be with his girlfriend." She was not the one to give up easily.

"Alright, but I can't locate his girlfriend anywhere," I said cautiously.

"Do you know who his girlfriend is?" she asked curiously.

"No."

"Then how the hell are you going to identify her? Did you dream about it?" she said. "Now, let's go. Don't create such a fuss."

I was not convinced, but still had to go in with her. In fact, this was the first time that I had entered any fashion store selling clothes for girls.

There were numerous mannequins sporting different fashion clothes. I was always fascinated by the designs and followed fashion closely, though I had never revealed it to anyone. I had always felt that that I had some sense of choosing the right colour combinations and choosing the right fabrics, but never got a chance to use that knowledge for a girl. I just followed Ruchita without showing much excitement. The times when I used to be excited about things were long gone.

After moving across the store a few times, she picked out a few dresses and skirts and asked me to wait outside the trial room. I felt my ears go red. Where was I stuck? I thought, feeling helpless. God knows where all the salesmen had vanished. I could see only salesgirls around me and I felt a bit embarrassed.

The door opened and she stepped out in one of the dresses she had picked. She asked, "How is it?"

"It's good," I said in a casual voice. The salesgirl who was also waiting outside with me walked towards her.

"Ma'am, how is the fit?" she asked politely.

"It's good enough," she replied without caring for her and instead looked at me.

Not having anything else to say, I asked her to try the other dresses too. I had nothing to do while she changed, so I started checking my WhatsApp messages. There was nothing important, so I looked around and waited. After many rounds of trial and error, she finally selected a blue skirt and paid the bill. I heaved a sigh of relief as we stepped out of the store.

It was almost 9 p.m. and I could still roam around for another hour. For some unknown reasons, I always preferred to be back to my room by 10 p.m. It was a rule that perhaps my mind had made subconsciously.

"Let's go and eat something. I am feeling hungry," she said making a puppy face. I nodded, finally happy at the ordeal having ended.

We went to the food court and ordered our choicest food. I asked her to occupy a good table while I waited at the counter to collect the order. With a tray in my hand, I searched for Ruchita once done. The food court was full of people and she was nowhere to be seen.

That's when I heard my name being called out loud. I turned back and saw Ruchita waving at me. I rushed towards her. She had managed to get a table for two and had kept her bag on the other chair in order to avoid any confusion with anyone. I put down the tray and sat down.

"Here's your chicken burger, cold drink and French fries," I said.

"Thank you, Mister Gentleman! Okay, tell me. When does a potato change it nationality?" she teased me, ripping apart the sauce packet with her teeth, and still somehow managing to giggle in between.

"What? What kind of a question is this? Nationality and a potato?" I asked, taking the burger out of the packet. I was too hungry to bother about anything else anyway.

"Think," she said with her mouth full of food.

"No, I won't. It's a stupid question." I took a bite of mine as well.

"See, again…you are a loser," she laughed again and then gulped down the chewed food to say, "It changes nationality when it becomes 'French' fries." And winked at me.

It wasn't funny, but the way she had said it made me laugh. I smiled at her innocence and stupidity. It made me go back in time. I remembered how I used to mock people at such questions and jokes, without once considering their feelings. When I started losing people and found that people had started distancing themselves from me, I realized how important it was to enjoy their conversations.

When I started laughing with Ruchita at her silly joke, I realized how much I had changed over the years.

I brushed those thoughts aside and asked, "So Ruchita, do you have a boyfriend?"

"No. I had one, but it didn't work out. So we broke up," she said coolly. "He was the biggest duffer I have ever seen. I wonder how I was even in a relationship with him to begin with. In fact, the guy before him was slightly better than him."

"Oh, so you have been in two relationships?" I mused.

"Yes. It worked for eight months with the first one and about ten months with the second one. Fuck, I couldn't even celebrate the first anniversary of my relationship with either of them, even though I was with two guys. You know the funny thing is, that the latest one didn't even know how to kiss. The one before that was definitely a better kisser than him." She saw my expression and laughed.

I had found the way she was narrating it hilarious and was surprised at how she was opening up. She was so casual about it and made it sound like it was some movie that she was talking about. She was laughing like crazy by now, so I laughed along.

Once the laughter had died down, I asked her, "So did you find a better kisser yet? Not seeing anyone?"

"Aah, not interested anymore," she replied, slurping her cold drink noisily. "It's tough to match the frequency of two people these days, and most of the guys I meet talk quite creepily. So it's better that I stay away from them. You know what…for any relationship to work, love acts as a binding factor, which is not so easy to find. Moreover, I find all these relationship things so idiotic. Initially it all begins with each other's happiness and smiles and good times, and then things start changing. It all eventually boils down to sex. So every day, it's either sex or sex. In my past relationship too, I was fed up with him. No more birthday surprises, no more fun and it becomes a kind of burden after a while." She finished and I was surprised at her frankness.

"Maybe," was all I could manage to utter.

She continued as casually as possible, "I can never understand one thing. If it's just about sex, why not just go to prostitutes and do whatever you want to? And you know the funny thing about my ex? He seemed like a maniac for physical pleasures, and he wasn't even good in bed."

I could only smile. I didn't know what else to say at that time. It was her personal experience that she was sharing with me over a meal. But I had no intentions to dig deeper into topics that I had no experience of. Yes, I knew guys who could not think of anything but sex – take Abhinav's case for instance – but I presumed that the girls involved would be getting equal pleasure out of it. It was mostly consensual, after all.

"Leave this fucking story of mine. Tell me more about you," she said and sipped the last drop of cold drink out of her glass. I just kept looking at her as she opened the cap of the disposable glass and peeped inside to see if there was any drop left.

I knew this question would come, so I was prepared. I looked at my wrist watch. Avoiding her questions, I said wiping my mouth with a napkin, "It's ten. Let's go. Your parents will be back soon."

"Yes, but at least tell me… Are you with someone or seeing anyone?" she asked once more.

"I will tell you some other day."

"Oh, what's so secretive?" she teased. "Okay, tell me a yes or no."

"Not now," I said and we left. We took a cab; I dropped her home before reaching my place.

I reached home and lay on the bed, looking at the fan again. But this time, the thoughts were positive. Gaurav had been right. A new chapter was about to begin, which would change the course of my entire life again.

My life seemed to have flipped over completely. With Vineet and Abhinav in the office and now Ruchita and a few others in the photography class, life seemed to be smiling upon me again. Clouds of depressing days were lifting. The only positive thing about bad times is that it always passes and so it was passing away for me too.

I had joined the photography classes to kill time and learn photography, and it felt great to be sharing it with Ruchita. She was full of life and had made me a part of hers too, a happy part at that. Life can take a flip if you are ready for that flip. With a smile on my face, I unlocked the room after dropping Ruchita home.

I messaged Ruchita to ask if she would join me for photography on Sunday at Humayun's Tomb as had been suggested by Ramesh. She promptly replied with a yes.

I looked around the room. It was a total mess. All my clothes were dirty and nothing seemed to be at its right place. I set out to make the room look decent, and put things in place. After completing whatever I could lay hands on to my satisfaction, I signed in to Facebook. There was a friend request waiting. Ruchita Narang. I accepted the request without another thought. I had just clicked on her name to see her profile in detail, when a Facebook message popped up.

'*Hi,*' Ruchita wrote.

'*I know what you are going to say,*' I replied. '*Hope I didn't surprise you much.*'

I was sure she would have seen my friends by now, and would have read comments on my book too. That's the first thing anyone would take note of in my profile and I hadn't even hinted at anything like that to her.

'*What the fuck man! You didn't say a word. I will kill you when we meet.*'

I just sent a wink smiley. I knew nothing could be said in my defense anyway.

'*Wait, let me at least hear your voice when I thrash you.*'

And my phone began buzzing, with her name flashing on the screen. I was prepared for the conversation, which eventually turned out to be seriously cute.

"Hey Ruchita. What's up?" I said as casually as I could.

"Shut up dude! First tell me why didn't you tell me that you are an author and have published a book?" She was still furious.

"I don't tell anyone about it yaar."

"But why? You know what, when I searched your name on Facebook, I saw an entire page to your name. I was so surprised and still was in doubt whether it was really you. When I checked your profile, it got confirmed. I can't believe you didn't tell me about this."

I tried to calm her down. "I don't feel like telling anyone about this. I wrote the book by chance, not as a passion."

"But dude, you have no idea what you have done. It's brilliant. And imagine if you did something by chance and it earned you so many admirers, what would happen if you plan and do such a thing? I am so excited to know this about you. I had no idea I was having all the fun these days with a goddamn famous author. I beat a celebrity in a golgappa eating competition. Oh gosh! I still can't believe it."

Now her words seemed overdramatic to me. "I am no celebrity. You are exaggerating, and pulling my leg. Aren't you?"

"Dude, you don't have any idea how famous you are. And anyway, tell you what, even if some silly guys get to publish their foolish articles in the local college magazine, they act like some celebrity columnist. I will give it to them in their face from tomorrow onwards, because a bestselling author is now my friend." She sounded so proud of me, and it gave me a sense of unparalleled happiness.

"But I don't understand why you don't talk about your book? It will give you the best publicity and it will sell more also," she said inquisitively.

"As I said, I am a writer by chance. What if people start asking me questions…I don't want that."

"Okay! That's a very silly reason, by the way. But now that I am your friend, I will do it for you. I will announce it in the next class. People will clap for you and I'll love to see it. "

"No Ruchita. You are not going to do anything of that sort," I said almost scared that the crazy girl would actually do it.

"Huh, we'll see about that. But before that, tell me one thing. Is it your story?"

"Kind of."

"Wow! I must read it then. I don't know why, but it feels like I have seen this cover and title somewhere. I don't remember where. I think I've even heard your name earlier somewhere, but I can't recall where. That's why when you told me your name, I felt that I had heard it somewhere. God knows."

"It happens." I was glad to have changed the topic. "There is no uniqueness in my name. It's common."

"Oh no, it is not. Well, I will find out. I am good at such snoopy kind of things. Big fan of Sherlock Holmes, you see!"

"Really? Wow, what a coincidence! Me too."

"Then between us, I will be Sherlock Holmes and since you write, then you can blog about it. So you will be Dr Watson."

I laughed at her innocence.

"Okay. So what's the code of the locker in the scandal of Bookland Revelation? Is it 36-24-36?" I joked, thinking this would shut her up for a while.

"Oh, just shut up! I know what you are hinting at, you cheapster! Let's see if you can find the code yourself."

"How would I? I am just Dr Watson. You are Sherlock Holmes. You have observatory powers. I don't interfere in your work."

"Oh god! Find something sensible to say, Sanjeev! You are sounding so silly," she mocked me playfully and I laughed it off.

"And listen," she quickly asked. "So we are going the day after tomorrow for the photography field practice, na?"

"Yes, you just confirmed that you will come along."

"Yes, I will be there at ten."

And we said goodnight to each other.

That night, I didn't have any dreams and I slept peacefully. I woke up in peace, neither panting, nor scarred by the thoughts that had kept me awake for so long. I realized that with Ruchita and her stupid acts, I was enjoying everyday life like I never had. Thanks to her, I found myself opening up to life and even being silly sometimes. I wasn't afraid of anything now.

I smiled and opened the window next to the bed. After such a long time, I saw the sun rise. I felt refreshed. I looked at the floor to locate my slippers when I happened to see my running shoes, lying ignored in a corner. With a smile, I slipped them on and went out to run till I exhausted myself. It was the perfect start to a day. I spent the entire day actively putting the room back in order, washing all the dirty clothes, rearranging the food items and throwing away the packed food that had run past its due date. At the end of the day, I was dead tired, but happy.

The next morning, the doorbell woke me up with its persistent ringing. I wondered who it could be so early in the day, because hardly anyone knew my address. I was lazily slithering out of bed, eyes still not opened fully, but the doorbell hadn't stopped ringing even for a second. I shouted "Coming…" and rushed to open the door.

Lo behold! It was Ruchita. I was in a vest, so I rushed back to pick up the t-shirt that was thrown on the chair. She was still at the threshold, looking at me with a strange expression on her face. I checked the watch; it was eight on a Sunday morning.

"Ruchita! What are you doing here at this hour? And how the hell did you find my address?" I said, rubbing my eyes, still wondering if it was a dream or was she really here.

"You want me to answer from here, or will you ask me to come inside?"

"Oh yeah! Needless to say…Come in," I said sheepishly, pointing at the chair for her to have a seat.

"So? What brings you here?" I asked once she had settled on the chair.

"Nothing! My dad had to go somewhere, and he asked me to drop him. He also allowed me to take the car for the photography practice. Since your room was on the way, I thought I'd pick you up. Simple!"

My eyebrows shot up. "All that's completely fine, but who gave you my address?"

"Are you underestimating my potential, Dr Watson? I am Sherlock, remember?"

"Yes, Lady Sherlock. Now will you answer me or have you answered it in your mind palace like Sherlock?" I quipped, making her smile.

"Nice, you're learning fast, I see!" She beamed and continued, "But why are you so curious about it? It's not so tough to get anyone's email id, phone number and address in this digital world."

"Oh, drama queen!"

"Okay, okay! I just got your address out from the photography class. I called up the reception. I wanted to surprise you... probably to see you half-naked." She chuckled.

"And?"

"And what? See, I surprised you and even saw you half naked." She giggled louder this time.

"Oh god! There's no beating your madness. You wait here. I'll just freshen up and then we will leave."

It took me around thirty minutes to get ready. I threw on a t-shirt and a pair of jeans. I saw her observing my room carefully when I came out. She had a copy of my book in her hands that she must have picked up from the bookshelf.

"Could you recall where you had seen my book then?"

"Yes, Dr Watson. I just went into my mind palace and remembered everything."

"Oh my my! You never leave a chance to show off. Do you?"

"Never! That's my favourite pastime," she said. Seeing my confused expression, she added, "Showing off, I mean!" Seeing the look on my face change from confusion to exasperation, she said, "It was one of my classmates who had read your book. She had brought the book to college once."

"Oh, nice. I hope he or she liked the book. But anyway, let's get going."

We came out of my apartment; with me holding the camera gear and she playing with the car keys. She had parked the car outside the building and when I saw the car, I was taken aback. Shocked would be an understatement; my mouth was open and I could just stare at the machine.

"Ruchita! You drive a Jaguar?"

"Yes! Dad's car."

I blinked and looked at her. "Oh, are you some rich spoiled kid from Defence Colony?" I teased.

"Rich? Yes, you can say that! Lots of money. Dad is a big shot lawyer. Touchwood. But spoiled? *You* tell *me*. What do you think?"

"I don't know. Hard to guess. But looking at the way you were devouring the golgappas that day, I couldn't even infer you are that rich," I said, and winked at her. She burst out into sweet laughter.

We settled in the plush car and she turned the key. The sound of the engine coming to life was in itself a treat to the senses. I can't even begin to explain how it felt to be sitting inside such a luxurious car with a girl driving me around.

I came back to the conversation that we had left midway at my room. "So where did your research go? Who was that reader you were talking about, Sherlock?" I asked.

"Aah, I haven't spoken to anyone about it yet, but yes, when I go to college tomorrow, I will surely do. But I am pretty sure that I saw your book in my college."

She switched the music player on with one swift push on the steering wheel somewhere.

We had reached well before time according to our calculation, since Ruchita had landed at my room pretty early, but still, some traffic had delayed us. Most of our classmates had already reached and were clicking pictures when we reached Humayun's Tomb. Ramesh was right there, instructing them about the exposure, lighting and composition of the pictures. We silently stood at the back of the group. Ramesh did see us, but continued with the lesson. After fifteen minutes of tutorial, he dispersed the crowd and instructed them to click as many pictures as they felt like. He had a habit of saying over and over again that the art of taking photographs isn't in knowing the settings of a camera, but in using them intelligently.

As we were about to leave with the others, Ramesh called out to us and said that he'd be around for about half an hour more and we could approach him for any help.

I started looking for an appropriate location and began clicking, while Ruchita went to another spot. For the next fifteen minutes or so, I struggled a lot with the lighting; most of my pictures were out of focus, or sometimes the background didn't blur. That reminded me of one of my friend's words: *"Dude, if the background isn't blurred, there is no point of having a DSLR."*

I went to Ramesh to understand the required settings, which he gladly explained. He left soon after, and everyone broke free to have fun. They started clicking portraits of each other for Facebook profile pictures. It was fun to see them. Amidst all this, I couldn't see Ruchita anywhere. I wondered where she could be and started looking for her. Humayun's Tomb is spread over a large area. I called her up and she picked up the call after a few rings. She whispered, "Come to the back of the tomb. Some fun is happening here."

I rushed towards the back side of the tomb, wondering what she could have meant. As I approached, I saw Ruchita hiding behind a pillar, trying to click pictures. I looked in the direction that the camera was working, but didn't find anything important. Ruchita saw me just then and waved to call me. As I reached near her, she whispered, pointing at something, "Look at the couple. Too busy kissing. They don't know what's going on around them."

I looked where she was pointing. A young boy and girl were too busy devouring each other, sitting behind a thick bush, feeling romantic under the blue sky like some Yash Chopra movie.

"So what? Don't you know how hard it is to get a room these days to make love? Leave them alone and let's click some beautiful photographs of the tomb."

"No, silly. I can't let such moments go so easily. Let's click their pictures."

"How cheap! Give them some privacy."

"Oh, holy man, the messenger of peace. This is what we call fun. And this is not just a good idea; it's an awesome idea."

Ruchita started clicking their pictures stealthily, but the camera does make some sound while clicking. It was a matter of a few moments when the lovers turned back and started shouting at us. Seeing this, we ran away from that spot and they started chasing us. I am sure they would have wanted to delete those pictures.

We didn't stop till we had reached the parking lot. They weren't behind us anymore. We looked at each other and laughed like crazy. What an adventure it was! That was the very first time that I had done something as silly as that in my life. I realized that Ruchita had the caliber to find fun in the strangest of things. The good thing now was – I was a part of it too.

The next day, Ruchita reached college in time for the most attended class. She wanted to ensure that most girls from the class were there so she could track the one in whose hands she had seen my book. She was trying hard to remember who it was, but wasn't sure from where she should begin her interrogation.

The class was finally over and she had had no luck. She was on her way to the library when she saw Isha. She thought since she had to start with someone, why not Isha!

"Hey, Isha," Ruchita called out.

"Hey Ruchita! Wassup?"

"Nice top yaar! Where did you buy this from?"

"Thanks. I got it from the Forever 21 outlet at Select City Walk mall."

"Oh, really? Why didn't you ask me? I would have loved to go there too." She shrugged, perhaps to indicate she couldn't do anything about it now. But this was just small talk; the real thing was yet to come. "By the way," Ruchita continued, "Do you remember, a few months back, someone was gaga about a novel in our college canteen. It had a reddish cover as far as I can recall."

"Yes. I think I know about that book," she said trying to think hard. "I guess it was Shuchi. But I am not too sure. You can ask her once." She was just about to scoot when she added, "I saw her going towards the canteen."

"Okay, and thanks. I'll see you in class."

Ruchita walked towards the canteen, happy to have gotten a lead. She saw Shuchi walking towards the college canteen with a group of girls. She called out to her. Shuchi looked back, stopped and asked the group of girls to go ahead when she saw Ruchita gesturing at her to stop.

Ruchita walked up to her and said, "Hi."

"Hi," she replied briefly. They weren't good friends, but knew each other by face.

"What's up?" Shuchi said, because she couldn't think of anything else to say.

"Nothing much…." Ruchita said and continued looking around, "Can we sit down somewhere?" She pointed towards a nearby stone chair.

Ruchita began without another thought. "I remember, a few months back, you were excitedly telling someone about a novel in class. I have never seen you so excited after your break-up. Though I can't remember the title of that book, I can deduce that you loved the book very much."

"*In Course of True Love.* That's the title."

"Yes, yes. Right." Ruchita was so excited to have been able to track her down in the first go.

"I remember Isha once mentioned that you always wanted to meet the author. You had even mailed to him, but nothing much happened. Is it true?"

"Yes. He replied to my email, but only once, that too the very first time when I mailed him. But never replied to my subsequent emails. I am sure he was busy to be answering every single mail. I loved the way he wrote the book. I got it from a bookstore close to my cousin's house when I went there last summer. I could easily relate to the story. I had so many questions to ask him, but he didn't seem interested," Shuchi said, stopped for a moment and continued, "Why are you asking me all this?"

"I have already read it. I am asking...," she took a pause to give a dramatic suspense, "because the author is my friend."

"What?" Shuchi jumped up hearing what Ruchita had just said. She seemed bewildered. "Unbelievable! How is that possible? Did you meet him?"

Ruchita smiled and nodded. Her eyes sparkled when she asked, "Can you please introduce me to him? How does he look? Is he just like he describes himself in the book?" She was as happy as someone would be on hitting jackpot. Her face turned red with happiness, and something else perhaps.

"Wait, wait! My god, so many questions in one go." She stopped as someone shouted out Shuchi's name. It was the same group of girls who were with Shuchi earlier. They were waving at her, but she shouted that she would see them in class and turned towards Ruchita.

"Please please, introduce me to him. You know very well how badly I have always wanted to meet him." Shuchi rattled off, as if not knowing what to do with the happy news she had just received.

"Yes, I will ask him and will let you know when we can meet. Sounds good?"

"Super!" She almost shouted and both stood up. They headed towards the class for the lecture – Shuchi looking forward to meeting Sanjeev, and Ruchita planning to arrange the meeting.

❀

Monday was a crazy day for me, Vineet and Abhinav. The weekend work load had all piled up and didn't even leave us time for our tea break. The only consolation was the photography class in the evening.

I wrapped up my work to be able to reach the class in time. I had already taken my fixed seat in the first row. When Ruchita entered the class, she wore a winning smile and I was left wondering what could be the reason. Perhaps she had found the fan. She came and sat beside me.

"Looking at the beaming face, seems like Miss Sherlock has solved the case," I poked.

"Yes!" She looked at me with pride in her eyes. "Details will be coming after the class."

That got me excited too.

In the meantime, Ramesh asked us to show him the photographs we had clicked at the Humayun's Tomb and simultaneously kept suggesting tips for the next time. My pictures still had quite a few drawbacks, but it surprised me to see that Ruchita's photographs were pretty awesome. Right colours and perfect angles.

"How come your photographs are so nice? You were so busy clicking lovers," I said surprised, yet impressed.

"My dear friend, showing that you work and really working are different things. But don't worry. Now that you're with me, you will get to know the reality of life." She winked in her signature style.

The class was soon over after we got some more tips on our individual work and style of working. When we came out, I asked her, "Are you going to tell me about the adventure of the fan or not?"

"Oh yeah! So like always, I was right. She is one of my seniors in college and a huge fan of you and your work. In fact, when I talked to her today, she made much noise out of excitement while talking about you and the book. She said she has emailed you a couple of times and you have responded once. Do you remember?"

"A lot of people write to me, so I cannot remember everyone. But tell me her name, at least. I will check the mail."

"Her name is Shuchi." She waited to see if the name would ring a bell, but it didn't. "So Mr Author, you are famous, man. Even in my college."

"Oh, come on! I am not famous…just that some people have read my work and liked it."

"Oh, modesty is old-fashioned. Keep it to yourself, otherwise how will you sell your books?" We had reached her car and she kept her camera and gear on the back seat. Before she turned the ignition, she lowered the window and said, "She really wants to meet you. Would you meet her? I promised her that I would ask you for her."

It took a few seconds for me collect my thoughts and speak. "Yes, I would love to. Can you ask her to email me once? I will connect with her."

"Are you feeling nervous?" She had a naughty smile on her face, clearly enjoying the moment.

"Yes, a little perhaps. I have hardly met any of my readers before this."

"She likes you, dude. She is very excited to meet you."

I checked my email and found an email from Shuchi waiting for me. That was quick, I thought and clicked on the email.

From<Shuchiverm.a@gmail.com>
To<sanjeev.ranjan91@gmail.com>

Hi Sanjeev,

I cannot even begin to tell you how happy I am today to hear about you from Ruchita. She told me everything about you. I had asked her to request you to meet me and you gladly said yes. I was a little angry at first because I had requested to meet you whenever you came to Delhi and you didn't even inform your fans, which includes me. You broke your promise, but no problem. I am so happy to think that we are meeting soon. I can't express this happiness. The more I read your book, the more I fall in love with its story. Please tell me where we are meeting and when.

Love,

Shuchi.

I was a tad bit surprised at the overwhelmingly happy email. It gave my morale a strong boost to see that someone had loved my work so much.

I replied:

From< sanjeev.ranjan91@gmail.com>
To<Shuchiverm.a@gmail.com>

Hi Shuchi,

Yes, Ruchita told me about you too. I am so happy to know that you loved my book so much. I am equally excited to meet you. How about this Sunday at Café Coffee Day in Connaught Place?

Regards,

S

She replied promptly:
Yayy! I will be there at 6 p.m. sharp. Even before time, maybe. I am so happy. Thank you, thank you, thank you. I am dancing in my room right now.

I smiled reading her excitement. Somewhere in my heart, I was excited to meet her; but in my mind, I was a bit nervous as well.

It was the first time I was going to be face to face with any reader, and I didn't want to disappoint her.

I took out a shirt that I had purchased ten months back. I wore it with a pair of denims and put on a blue jacket. There was a blue blazer also. This was the first time I had worn this combination. I looked out of the window, and I could sense that there was a nip in the air. I looked at myself in the mirror, pretty happy with how I was looking. I even practiced to smile a few times looking at myself in the mirror, as I was accused of having a bad first impression. Perhaps smiling a bit would not make me look arrogant and stiff, as most friends had complained to me of late.

As is my habit, I was at the designated place much before the scheduled time. I looked around, but didn't see her. I remembered that she had said in one of the emails that she'd be wearing a red jacket. I looked around again, and to my horror, many girls wore red jackets! Perhaps it was a hot trend or something. So I decided to wait. She must have seen my picture in the author's bio on the back cover. She would recognize me if I did not. I went inside the café and took the corner seat.

I kept looking at the entrance every now and then, but no hint of her so far. Twenty minutes passed. I kept fiddling with the menu to while away some time. But when I raised my head to look at the entrance again, I saw a girl, standing near my table…smiling. I looked at her for a moment before she parted her lips and said, "Sanjeev?"

"Yes," I replied with a smiling face and stood up, putting forth my hand for a handshake.

She didn't blink for a few seconds, as if she had seen some ghost. Or a celebrity perhaps, I thought reminded of Ruchita's words.

Celebrity? Me? Oh, not at all. I have written just one book, that too not so popular. Sold only about ten thousand copies in the last three years. Yes, she had loved the book, but still, it doesn't qualify me as a celebrity.

When every wild conjecture of mine for having been stared at was ruled out foolishly, I glared at her. She kept gazing at me without speaking a single word. With passing time, I started finding it awkward as I wanted both of us to take our seats before the staff and others around started thinking we were a bunch of crazy youngsters. Since she was not taking the initiative, I thought of taking the first step and said, slowly, "Hi."

She, with a very big smile on her face, uttered her first word, which sounded perfectly sweet. "Hi"

Somewhere, it really felt good to be recognized and respected like this, but things could have turned awkward again with the way she was beaming and staring at me without blinking. So I took an initiative again and said, "Shall we take our seats?"

She nodded like a doll with the same big smile that didn't seem to be fading.

Her eyes were big, with a perfect combination of eyelashes and kohl, which accentuated her look like a doll. Fair skin, glowing because of make-up and pinkish lips stood like a perfect curve of her face. Her teeth caught my attention as she had been staring at me, open mouthed. This was the first time that I had met someone who had such perfectly ordered teeth. She was the kind of girl whom I had often seen in expensive lounges, dating some rich guys. The kind of girl that every average guy wanted to date, but knew that it was out of bounds. Since it wasn't a date for me, I wanted to see the entire episode as an author-reader meet. So I wanted to act formally, though I am not a very formal person otherwise.

Just then, I recalled Abhinav's lines that I didn't have to sound desperate or needy. I had heard elsewhere also that if you talk too much with the person who admires you, you stand a high chance of losing your charm.

"What would you like to have? Latte or Cappuccino...or – cake with chocolate sauce? It's kind of my favourite," I asked shyly.

"Your favourite, of course. Chocolate sauce is coincidently my favourite too."

I signaled at a waiter and placed the order.

"So, yeah. Ruchita said that you were eager to meet me. I generally don't meet people as an author, but since you were so eager, I agreed. So tell me... I am sure you have things to talk about, right?"

She nodded again.

For the last several months, I had made it a habit to not speak much with unknown people, specifically about my books and personal life. I only wanted to share these details with people whom I considered quite close.

She folded her hands on the table, as if to control her excitement. "I want to know so many things about you and your book, but I know if I ask so many questions, you would get bored and irritated."

I assured her that I was not going to do anything of that sort. "Do you remember my email? I sent mails to you so many times. I was so mad about your book and for you. You were so cute in the novel." She giggled.

Before I could say a word, she quickly added, as if to herself, "I still can't believe I'm sitting right in front of you. Right. In. Front. Of. You. I have to tell you this. I have imagined this in my head so many times. I always thought what I would say, what I would do, how it would all turn out to be. I have looked forward to this meeting very much, honestly. My mom also knows, because I couldn't stop praising you and your book."

I smiled humbly, planning to tell her how elated I was to hear her talk like this, when she started talking again.

"Are you writing another book? I am so excited."

I put up both my hands, as if in defense and got all her attention almost immediately. "As of now, no. I haven't thought of writing another book."

"Oh, come on! You can tell me the truth. I won't reveal it on social media or to anyone. Promise!" she said innocently.

I laughed and shook my head, saying, "There's nothing like it, Shuchi. I don't yet have a story in my mind and heart for it."

She nodded before saying, "You know, I've read your book thrice so far. I read it often."

I was impressed. "Thrice? Really? That's amazing. I am really glad you liked it so much. I didn't know just a desperate attempt to lessen my pain through the character of Aarush would be so well received by readers."

She gazed at my face, and her expressions just before she asked the next question were many. As if she had had something in her mind for long which was desperately waiting to come out, and now she had released the arrow with the question. "Do you still love her?"

I looked at her surprisingly, because we both knew that these kinds of questions were quite uncomfortable to answer. Her face had the kind of look which would turn either happy or sad depending on the answer. I pondered over it, but she made it easy when she said, "I am really sorry. I shouldn't have asked this question. I was just overwhelmed to see the person who loved someone so truly, but didn't get the same love in return."

I wondered how she had understood me so well just on the basis of the book. I didn't know if other readers would have thought the same way, but the sensitivity with which she had read my pain was amazing. I brushed her uneasiness aside. "It's fine. You don't need to be sorry for this."

She smiled and said, "Then I would assume that you have moved on."

I quickly switched the topic by asking, "So…how is your college going?"

"It's pretty good. From now onwards, it's going to be super awesome. I am going to talk about our meeting to everyone in the college. Kind of bragging, you know."

"I don't think our meeting has been so awesome till now that you brag about it. You didn't find it boring?"

"No, why would I? You are still cute, just like in the book. You are one of the best listeners one can have, listening to my questions so patiently and even answering them. And since you haven't asked anything else apart from answering, I gather you're a bit shy. I find that extremely cute. I can observe you blushing at times. What more would I want to make this meeting interesting and worthy of bragging?" She was beaming as if she had proven her point.

"I don't know. A Delhi girl always prefers either hot guys or cool guys. Quiet ones like me feel rather intimidated," I opened up slightly, more for self-assurance than anything else.

"Not all Delhi girls are the same, you know!" She looked at me so adorably that I started feeling more and more comfortable.

"You are too kind," I said with a smile stretching from one ear to the other. I was happy.

"And you know you are too cute and sweet. Otherwise I know a few people who become famous and show attitude like they're some bigshot celebs. You talk so sweetly…you're so down to earth." She took the last bite of her cake and said, "I am going to make my friends jealous by telling them that my favourite author asked me out for coffee, and it was one of the best meetings ever." She winked.

"Asked you out? Isn't it just a little bit of exaggeration?" I didn't really mind if she bragged about me; I was just having a nice conversation with a stranger after long, and loving it.

"Not at all. Remember, I have your email as proof where you've said that we can meet over coffee." She laughed victoriously, and I could only smile. She was right.

Just then, my phone vibrated. There was a WhatsApp message from Abhinav.

Aha! Meeting a girl. That's why you keep silent when Vineet and I fight over the topic of girls. I am right behind you, two tables apart.

I turned around to see Abhinav grinning like a devil.

"Is it someone you know?" asked Shuchi.

I hastily thought of the most appropriate thing to be done and blurted, "Would you mind if we leave for now? We can meet later sometime, and I promise I will answer all your questions."

"Yeah. Sure," she said, but her eyes reflected a certain disappointment.

"Thanks. I can drop you," I offered, being my chivalrous self.

She stood up, picking up her bags. "It seems like I have freaked you out," she said hesitantly.

"No, you haven't! It's just that this is the first time I am meeting someone like this…you know, nothing of this sort ever happens with me that…"

Before I could complete the sentence, Shuchi interrupted, "But I am sure you have interacted with many. Your Facebook page is flooded with posts."

"Yes, sometimes. But that doesn't involve a face to face rendezvous, does it?"

She merely smiled and I asked her, "How are you planning to go home?"

"I will take an auto, don't worry. See you again soon."

We walked out together and she got an auto easily. I bade her goodbye and watched her leave, till the auto disappeared from my sight.

I bought a few essentials for my working kitchen at home on my way back. I had resolved to have a healthy regime and wanted to try some healthy alternatives to outside food. I was carrying quite a few bags and managed to open the lock with great struggle. Hands full, turning the key with a single finger, pushing the door open with the elbow, and running towards the chair to unload myself – it was an adventure in itself.

I was hungry by now, so I quickly freshened up and ate my tiffin. When I had settled down in bed for the night, I logged into my Facebook account. There were more than twenty notifications; Shuchi had been liking all my recent posts on Facebook.

A message popped up on my screen. Shuchi was asking, *'You reached home?'*

'Just a few minutes back. You tell me, reached safely?' I asked.

'Nope, I was kidnapped on my way back. I was getting bored so the kidnapper lent me his laptop. :P'

'Oh come on! This is not something to joke about.'

'Writing is quite tough, isn't it?' She suddenly changed the topic of our conversation and I couldn't ignore it, because this was a reader asking an author.

'Yes, but that's not something I can explain on chat.'

'*So how about meeting up again?*' she asked suddenly and I was left dumbfounded.

'*Sure,*' I typed hesitantly.

'*Great, tomorrow evening, after your office perhaps? There is a park near my home. I am sure the author in you will get inspired with all the beauty nature has to offer.*'

'*Sounds like a plan. But can we make it day after? I have my photography class.*'

'*Oh yeah, I am so sorry I totally forgot. Ruchita had told me about it. Let's make it day after then. ☺*'

'*Okay.*'

I was happy that we would be meeting again. In her I had found a good friend in the very first meeting. I knew the second one would be great too.

'*I will get going, mom's calling. See you soon. Good night. I will send you the location on WhatsApp. Will that be okay?*'

'*Oh yes.*'

The next two days passed in the anticipation of meeting her, and we continued to chit chat over Facebook chat and WhatsApp on Monday too. Abhinav had grilled me in office on Monday, and Ruchita had her share of fun at the photography class in the evening. But I didn't mind it much; my thoughts were clean and I knew they were just teasing.

On Tuesday, I was in unusually high spirits. While Abhinav and Vineet believed it was perhaps the 'girlfriend', I was just happily looking forward to a good evening.

After leaving office, I headed straight to the park where Shuchi had asked me to meet her. When I reached, she was waiting for me at the gate itself. We walked in together and took the elevated path made for walkers and joggers.

After asking how my day had been and other casual things, I saw that Shuchi had turned serious all of a sudden and asked me, "So you had to tell me if writing is tough. You couldn't explain it in words on chat the other day, remember?"

"You're still there, I see! Honestly, umm…" I thought for a moment and said, "I found writing tough. Listening to yourself amid all the noise and muffled voices all around you is tough. Very tough at times. But why do you ask?"

"Hmm. You know, once I had written an article for the college magazine. It took me a week to draft the article. And can you believe, despite my having put in so much time, the review was the worst you can imagine. Hardly anyone liked it. So I can easily say weaving such a long story with each and every word to make sense would be quite tough." She smiled beautifully, making me feel like a celebrity.

"Yes, it takes time for sure."

"So do you write daily?"

"I am not writing anything these days. I write when I feel like writing. When the voice actually comes from my heart. Otherwise I find my emotions artificial."

"That's what I love about you. Your words show your emotions in a real way. Your story almost made me drown in the sea of the world you had created. The way you think defines you. Isn't it?"

"I don't know. I have never thought about this. What defines you?"

We came to a wooden bench while walking and sat down. There were many couples roaming around, kids playing in the patches where the grass had withered, and some older people walking and jogging on the tracks.

She looked into the distance and spoke with sweet severity, "Life has been so adventurous that it can't be explained. We meet people all the time, and not always with a particular aim that we have to be friends with them. But, they just come along and it's good to have them along. They are good individually, but having all of them together at the same time seems like chaos. It's just like having beautiful stones separately, but having them together makes it look like an ordinary dump. I don't want dump. I don't like such chaos. I never knew that I will have to 'manage' my friends too. I want to be with one person at a time and give him or her all my attention. That is why I don't like technology. It has given us pace, which was never required. Not in relationships, at least. The world is all sci-fi today. I don't like it like that. I want a simple place with simple people. I want things to be gradual and peaceful."

She was looking ahead at no one in particular, but continued talking.

"I like the chirping of birds. I hate discos. I like the breeze. I hate the AC. The sci-fi world suffocates me. I don't just want to move forward, I want to fly. I want it all to go a little slow. The happiness around us demands to be felt now and guess what? I don't have time for it." And then she stopped as abruptly as she had started. There had been an ecstasy on her face when she had been talking.

I thought for a while over what she had said and didn't know what to say. I was impressed at how naturally and effortlessly she had shared something that actually needed so much of effort and guts to even acknowledge to oneself. Listening to her voice had a soothing effect, for it had the coaxing inflections of a child. Her face reflected that she had spilled everything that was in her heart for so long. It was quite evident that she wasn't just pretty, but very beautiful deep within too. I fixed my gaze appraisingly upon her. I hadn't understood what she meant by her last line though.

Her reverie broke and she looked at me, somewhat embarrassed.

"Woah, those were some deep thoughts. I have felt like that sometimes," I said to fill the silence.

"Really? I have never shared this with anyone else."

"Yes, definitely." I said, reassuring her. I was struggling to keep this conversation going unphilosophically, because whenever such things come up, my mind becomes full of philosophical thoughts and then conversations tend to become boring and people feel left out. So I chose not to express myself right then, but yes, I noted a few things in my mind silently. *Birds chirping, not liking AC, loving breeze, peace around self as the world is too sci-fi.*

We both didn't talk for a while, and let the silence do the talking. Shuchi suddenly got up and began walking towards some unknown path, in a zigzag manner. I was still wondering over her words. Plus, it was getting dark too. I wanted to ensure she reached home in time and safely.

"Where do you live?" I asked her.

"I live close by, not very far from this park. We can walk down to my place."

"Yes, sure. I would prefer to drop you before I head home. After all, chivalry is not dead," I said with a smile.

She smiled back ever so sweetly. "Where do you live?" she asked me.

"Hauz Khas. I will take the metro from here. Shouldn't take much time."

We walked together for about fifteen minutes, through so many turns and alleys. We spoke of random things, perhaps to balance out on the heavy dose of philosophy. Then slowly, Shuchi stopped in front of a house. It was big, painted fully in white.

"This is my house," she said sweetly.

"Oh, it's as beautiful as you," I remarked earnestly.

"Thanks." She blushed and continued, "And thanks for spending time with me. I enjoyed it." She paused, hesitant to put in words what her heart and mind had been telling her. "Umm, I find you very sweet and really like you." Saying this, she quickly turned towards the gate.

"Wait, I am glad you said that. I enjoyed your company too." Then, just to tease her I said, "Aren't you going to invite me inside?" I wanted to prolong this conversation for a few minutes more, so dropped the ball in her court.

"I wish I could. Some other day for sure." She came towards me with a scintillating smile and gave me a hug. I was happy and felt like jumping with joy. She gave me a peck on my cheek and turned towards her house.

I stood there, waiting to let what had happened sink in. Within a second, she had walked back into her house.

When I reached home, I was happy. I freshened up and had my dinner, with a smile pasted on my lips. Her face hovered in front of my eyes, the usual smile adorning her. I loved her smile; so bright and soothing to my soul. It was the kind of smile that makes you hopeful that someone is interested in talking to you and knowing more about you. It makes your jaded heart calm. It appeared to me that she smiled a lot because of me, seeing me, and it always gave me unexpected warmth; something I had been looking for endlessly.

When Shuchi walked into the living room through the main door, she saw her mom gazing at her lovingly, as if she had been waiting for her.

"Hey Mom! What are you doing here?" she said, keeping her bag on the side table. "It seems you have been waiting for me."

"Yes, my dear. Who else do I have in this life to look forward to except you?" she said, gesturing at Shuchi to sit beside her on the sofa.

"How was your day?" asked her mom, caressing her hair.

"It was good." She was wondering whether to share with her mother her feelings about Sanjeev.

Her mother waited a while and then broke her silence. "Don't you want to share anything about the new person with whom you were standing outside?"

"Oh, you saw him?" she said, not able to control the crimson blush that came up automatically.

"Why? Am I not supposed to see him? Or were you planning to hide him or something?" her mother asked with a gentle smile, knowing well that her daughter would never hide anything from her.

"Mom, stop teasing me. You know very well that I don't hide anything from you." Her mother nodded. "I thought I'd tell you a little later, you know. Well, he is Sanjeev."

"Seems like I have heard this name somewhere."

"Yes. He is the author of *In Course of True Love*."

"Oh yes! I remember how excited you were after reading the novel and the whole week you were talking about it," her mother said smiling.

"He is my college friend Ruchita's friend. They are together in the photography class." Her mother looked happy, so she continued. "You know, I was so eager to meet him ever since I had read the book. So Ruchita asked him to meet me and he agreed. Wasn't that sweet of him?

"Yes, it was very kind of him. And how did my sweet daughter find him?"

"He is different. I mean, he is not like other guys. I don't know why, but I shared something with him that I couldn't have the courage to share with anyone. And he understood it; he said it was quite deep. I felt good that someone had understood me so well."

"I am so happy for you, my baby. After so many months, I have seen you so happy. He has come into your life like a gift, hasn't he?"

"Well, you can say that. But he doesn't speak much."

"He has already spoken a lot through his novel. He is a heart-broken person, it seems, and for such people, it's tough to express again. Wasn't it the same for you till a few months back?"

"Mom, have you also read the book? You know so much," Shuchi was surprised.

"What do you think? My daughter keeps talking about something for a day, in fact, for a week. I had to read it."

Shuchi looked at her, but didn't say anything. Her mom continued, "Shuchi, can I ask you something?"

"Yes, mom?"

"Do you like him?"

Shuchi didn't want to answer this.

"I am asking you something, beta. Tell me honestly."

"I think so, mom. I like spending time with him. In fact, today when he came to drop me, I wanted to invite him in, but couldn't say this to him. He even asked, though teasingly, if I was going to invite him inside. I didn't. I think I hurt him."

"No, you didn't hurt him. Your intention wasn't to hurt him, and if your intention is true, things will remain fine. I know what happened between you and that guy. I remember everything, but you really need to give life a second chance. I think he knows how it feels to hurt someone, because he has been hurt himself. Like you, he is also suffering from the burden of memories, but just think about him once. Because of Rohan, you were so broken that you didn't even go to college for several months. Think about his pain. He had to write the book to lessen the pain that was tormenting him daily. Don't you think so?"

"You are right. He even said to me that he wrote the book for personal catharsis. That's why it felt so real while reading it. But sometimes I am surprised that you say these things after what happened between you and Dad. Don't you feel scared of it? I mean, this love and relationship business."

"That's what I have been teaching you, haven't I? What happened between me and Dad is a different thing. Sometimes we don't understand the person, no matter how many years we spend together; and sometimes you start feeling comfortable from the very first day. Initially, in any relationship, you will see that both feel happy and excited about their togetherness. It doesn't mean that both of them are necessarily in love. The initial phase is mostly clouded with attraction. Love happens when you both don't need to compromise for each other and feel comfortable in front of each other in any situation. You don't need to demand anything; if the other is not giving it freely, it's not worth it. There was no love between me and your Dad. We both misunderstood our attraction as love and got married. But when reality hit us, we started finding faults in each other. What I inferred after that is that love is a binding force between two people. It is this understanding, trust and respect for each other that drives a relationship for a long time." She paused and smiled to say, "Don't compare that to anything you go through in life. Take it as a lesson perhaps, but nothing else. And do invite him home the next time. I would love to meet him."

"Sure, mom."

"Let's have dinner. I am starving."

They ate together and watched a movie on the television. Her mom retired to her room thereafter and Shuchi was left to delve into her feelings.

She recalled that she had been in class 10 when her dad had left her and her mother and filed for a divorce. Shuchi's mom was keen on settling the matter after her board exams, but her father didn't listen to her. It so happened that everything got settled just before the board examinations were to begin. It was quite a tough time for her mom, but being a strong lady and having a job at a nationalized bank, she managed the situation single-handedly, without taking any help from the relatives. There had been times when Shuchi had seen her mom awake in the dead of the night, sitting in her chair like she was lost in thoughts.

She didn't even realize when she drifted off to sleep, appreciating her mother's will and dreaming of the good times to come.

The best kind of meeting with anyone is where you both don't need to put effort to meet each other. It was happening with Shuchi. Neither of us compromising on our office or study to meet.

A few days later, when we met casually while taking our customary long walk in the same park where we generally used to meet, Shuchi broke the silence.

"Okay, tell me something." She asked excitedly and I nodded. "Tell me about your perfect day."

"Perfect day? What do you mean by perfect day?" I was confused, not able to fathom what was it that she wanted to know.

"A perfect day... When you feel great, right from the moment you wake up, till you go to bed happily, without any worry and you get very good sleep. When at the end of the day you say to yourself, 'What a great day it was!'."

I thought for a second, but shook my head in a no. "Umm. I can't remember any such day," I replied in a normal tone. Listening to this, the brightness of her face dulled a bit, but she held herself immaculately.

"Have you ever had one?" I asked, wishing to know if I was the odd one out.

"I have never had one either, but I am looking forward to it," she said and I smiled. She continued, "But I guess I am about to get one soon."

I looked at her, a bit surprised. I wondered how she could be so sure of something that hadn't happened yet. She walked closer to me. She had a mischievous smile on her face, and came quite close to me. Then she whispered into my ear, "Thank you.

Every day with you is turning out to be a perfect day for me."
She reached up to my cheek and placed a gentle kiss.

It was quite unexpected. She was so close I could smell her
perfume. I just loved her fragrance, like I was passing through a
valley of flowers. I turned my head towards her and found her
lips just a few millimeters away from mine. I was hesitant to
move forward, but before I could understand, her lips met mine.
A few moments later, she pulled herself away. I was dazed.

I could see panic on her face when she suddenly increased
her pace and started walking away hurriedly.

I came to my senses and followed her, calling her name
from behind. She stopped and we let the awkward moment
pass. We walked back, crossing the small streets.

When we reached the gate this time, she didn't say goodbye.
She invited me in. I thought she was pulling my leg, but she
said she meant every word. After confirming with her twice, I
went in. She said her mom would be home soon, as she was out
to meet someone.

I entered hesitantly and noticed that the house had been
nicely done up. It was tastefully decorated and emanated
warmth of love from every nook. Shuchi went in to make coffee
for us, and I began looking around.

There were so many certificates perfectly framed in glass
hanging on one of the walls. I walked close to it and looked at
each of the certificates carefully. Most of them highlighted the
names of several competitions, some of them music events. My
mind registered she was a music lover. Other certificates were
of student councils. She had been the president of a student
council in the first and second year of college consecutively. By
the time I ended checking every certificate and painting that
adorned the wall, she walked in with two cups of coffee.

"Oh, inspecting my laurels like a spy?" she asked, chuckling.

"Oh, no no. I wasn't checking. I was just going through your laurels. Really impressive."

She laughed, handing me the mug of coffee.

"Are you still holding all these positions?"

"Nope," she said with her eyes downcast.

"Why?"

"I don't feel like doing anything of this sort anymore."

"And why is that?" I asked sipping the coffee.

"I'm not ready perhaps."

We sat on the sofa, facing the TV. I leaned forward and said, "This is really nice coffee. Far better than CCD." I was trying to lighten the situation, which had been made serious with my questions.

She smiled and nodded as an acceptance, but didn't utter a word.

I continued, "I saw one certificate from a music event. Do you play some music instrument as well?"

She nodded.

"And that is?"

"Piano."

"Wow! That certificate was from long back. Do you still play the piano?" I asked, almost finishing my coffee.

"No," she said slowly. She sat back. It seemed to me that she wasn't in the best of her moods.

"You know, I always wanted to learn to play the piano, but somehow couldn't get an opportunity."

"Why not now?" She looked at me. It wasn't the kind of look that would say 'leave me alone', but rather something painful that was breaking her from inside. I was puzzled to see that look on her face and wanted to hug her. Take her in my arms and kiss her on the forehead. Tell her that I am here and everything would now be fine. But I could not gather the guts to do that. Not yet. She had let me into her house, and I wasn't the one to take advantage.

I happened to look at the wall clock and realized it was getting late. I wanted to return to the room in time and waiting for aunty didn't make much sense. So I bade goodbye to Shuchi and asked her to cheer up. I left, but not without a promise to meet again soon.

Days passed and I began to see life afresh with Shuchi. Every day spent together was an occasion. I had been home with Shuchi a couple of more times too, for she made wonderful coffee and I was a fan. During one such meeting, I had met her mother. She seemed every bit like the strong woman that Shuchi had told me about. She was more like a one-woman army, full of great ideas and love for Shuchi, a part of which came to me as well.

Finally the day came for which I had been waiting ever since I had asked about it. Shuchi's birthday. 24th August. I wanted to make it the most memorable birthday for her, but how? I had been thinking about it for a long time, but hadn't been able to find a suitable way. Yet. The worst thing of all, that very day my amazing office decided to transform into a mean one, and I got stuck in office till eleven in the night. I was so furious at my manager for overloading me with so much of work that day; especially when I would have gladly agreed to it on any other random day.

I was embedded deep in my work, but still, every now and then, I couldn't avoid looking at my watch. I had wished Shuchi over phone and had apologized for not being able to meet her on the special day. She had not complained, saying that she knew how hectic offices could sometimes be, but I could sense the disappointment in her voice. She was trying to be cooperative, and I was trying to hurry up. But the work didn't finish before eleven. I had thought of going home to wish her, but it was too late for that too. Plus, I wasn't sure what could have been done at this hour. So I thought of ordering a cake and flowers online for midnight delivery. That way I stood a chance.

By the time he reached his flat, it was already half past eleven. He had just thrown his bag on the bed in exasperation and frustration when his phone rang. It was Ruchita.

"Hey Sanjeev. What's up?"

"Hi Ruchita. Nothing yaar, just reached home."

"Oooh, so how was the birthday party? I bet you got late there," she said trying to tease me.

"I wish that was the case. I was stuck with some stupid work that my stupid manager had assigned to me. I could barely take time out."

"Oh no! I guess all reporting managers are the same everywhere. Fucking retards! May his pants overflow with crawling insects that bug him to madness."

I couldn't resist laughing listening to her words.

After a moment, I said, "I couldn't plan anything in the office yaar. So I just ordered a cake and flowers to be delivered to her address." I was disappointed and in a way helpless too.

"Oh, don't be sad." She went quiet for a while. "Let's do something...Wait, let me think."

"What can be done at this hour? I so hate my job I cannot even tell you. I think…"

"Shoo. Don't talk. I am thinking," she ordered and I followed her majesty's orders.

"Let's go to her house and wish her!" Her voice brimming with excitement.

"Don't you think your Sherlock Holmes mind is getting crazy ideas these days? Her house? At this hour? Are you mad?" I discarded her idea before it could tempt me. I was a bad idea; if someone saw us, she could get into a whole lot of trouble. What would her mom think of me?

"Come on, you shouldn't behave like such a bore. It would be so much fun…just think about it. Plus, she would love to see you. I am telling you."

I didn't say anything. I was tempted, honestly, because I really wanted to see her and wish her. In the meantime, she continued, "Don't you think it would be super romantic to wish her looking into her eyes, holding her hands?"

"Oh, shut up!" I chided her, but this was all I needed to hear to get going. "But how will we go there?"

She laughed for a moment before saying, "Don't worry. I will pick you up. Then we will go together."

That gave me some hope. "Cool! Then let me talk to the cake and flower delivery customer care boy to not deliver the stuff and wait for me outside the house."

She quickly hung up and left the house to pick me up. We had twenty minutes in hand. I quickly changed into a pair of jeans and a t-shirt, and waited for Ruchita to come. I got her call within the next five minutes and rushed downstairs to head towards Shuchi's home. It was a kind of thrilling for me, for I hadn't done anything of this sort before.

We stopped at a distance from her house, seeing a security guard at the gate. I was anyway feeling awkward, so asked Ruchita, "What if the security guard doesn't let us in?"

"Don't worry about that. You wait here for the delivery boy and let me talk to the security guy. I will fix something up so he can let us sneak in."

"Okay, good idea," I said coming out of the car.

She parked the car outside the gate and headed towards the guard. Shuchi's house wasn't very far from the main gate.

I was looking at Ruchita talking to the security guard, not moving my gaze, just in case she needed my help for negotiation. Just then, I heard the sound of a roaring motorcycle, steadily increasing. I looked to one side and saw the delivery guy approaching the main gate. So I ran and stopped him before he could go in.

"Wait, wait!" I stopped the boy and he skid to a halt immediately.

"Where are you going?" I asked him.

He looked at me strangely and said, "Sir, to deliver a cake and a flower bouquet ordered by Mr Sanjeev."

"I am Sanjeev. Hand it over to me," I said. "I had called the customer care number to tell them that I'd be collecting the stuff myself. The payment is already done, so just tell me where to sign."

He nodded and got my signature on his long list before leaving the place.

I stood there looking at Ruchita haggling with the guard; from the way she was looking worked up, I presumed things weren't going per plan. A couple of minutes later, Ruchita came to me, looking dejected and angry.

"What happened?" I asked, hoping it wasn't what I was thinking it was.

"That stupid security guard won't let us enter at this hour, until he confirms by calling them. If he calls, the plan will flop. So I asked him to not call and said we will come tomorrow morning."

"I have come with Shuchi a couple of times, but it wasn't this guard then. Maybe the duties change at night or something. If it had been him, I would have still tried my luck."

She had not paid any attention to my words, it seemed. She was on her own trip. Perhaps this was the rare time when she hadn't been able to convince a guy to do her bidding, I mused. "And you know what, when I stopped him from calling them, you should have seen the look on his face. Like we are ethical burglars, taking permission for burglary. Loser!" Her face was almost crimson with anger.

I laughed and consoled her. "What now?"

She thought for a moment before saying, "Now, there's only one option left for us."

I raised my eyebrows to ask what she had in mind. "You have to climb the wall," she said casually as if she was talking about me eating an ice cream.

"What? No! You are totally mad, Ruchita. I will get caught and get beaten up for nothing. You have the car, and you will just drive away in case of any mishap. I will be caught and handed over to the police."

"Nothing of that sort will happen. You worry too much, dude. Let me park the car just beside the wall, so that you can climb on it and jump onto the other side. I will pass over the cake and flower once you're there. Sounds good?"

Honestly, I wasn't sure at all. This was the worst idea I had heard in ages. Even worse than what Abhinav often came up with to woo various girls. But then, I thought of sharing a moment together with her, looking into her eyes in the moonlight, sparkling and illuminating with shyness. Just a single thought of her saccharine smile convinced me to take this risk.

I was already convinced when Ruchita further cemented the resolve by saying, "Oh, don't think much. I will go along with you if you want. Plus, I will call my dad in case you get caught. He will defend you in court." She winked.

"Ha ha ha. How funny, Miss Sherlock." I looked at the wall and asked, "Will you ask her to open the balcony door?"

"Why balcony?" she said confused. "You can just ring the bell and enter the house."

"Yes, sure. Just a small problem – her mom will ask questions about my being here at this hour, and the poor guard will lose his job. I don't want all that now."

"Isn't it getting too adventurous?" She rubbed her hands in delight and said devilishly. She was deriving pleasure out of my plight, which would soon turn into my happiness if the plan succeeded.

"I think I will take a risk, now that your dad is ready to defend me in court," I joked.

"Oh, hero! You know how much he charges for a case?" she said with her hands resting on her waist.

"I don't know the fees, but I know his daughter. She will waive it for me." I winked this time.

She parked the car beside the wall. I climbed over, took the cake and flowers from her and whispered, "I can't hold the cake and flowers and climb up; something out of the two will fall and get ruined. Do you have something I can tie these up with?"

"Let me look in the car." She began checking the car. She found the engineering drawing drafter in the back seat. She hastily emptied it and gave the cover to me. I kept the flower bouquet in it and hung it on my back. I looked like some super hero with a quiver on his back. I looked around, and seeing no security guards in sight, jumped onto the other side. "Thank god, the wall wasn't that high," I whispered to myself.

The white light piercing the night mostly came from two or three windows opposite him, where people had still not gone off to sleep. But how would I recognize the window from the side? I was at the back of the house, since the front was manned by guards. There were no house numbers etched on the windows. I moved silently; I couldn't see much as a very dim light from the windows was filtering through the leaves. I took my phone out and turned on the torch in my mobile phone. I looked up to the three windows above me and my eyes searched for Shuchi. "Where is she?" I said to myself. When I couldn't see her, I got irritated with Ruchita. Did she even call Shuchi? I looked at my watch. It was almost twelve.

I kept looking up at the windows, hoping she would appear at some window and I would be able to wish her somehow. I was confused, to say the least, but hopeful nonetheless. Suddenly I could see some movement from the corner of my eyes. Someone was standing near a window waving at me. My face lit up when I saw Shuchi standing at the window.

"Sanjeev, up here, you silly boy," Shuchi said in as hushed a tone as possible.

How do I go upstairs? How do I give her the roses I had so lovingly ordered for her? I was pondering when I saw Shuchi pointing at something. I noticed that there was a small spiral staircase, perhaps used as a service staircase from the back of the houses. Most of the houses were linked to the staircase with a common platform, a small door from each house opening up onto the platform. I looked at her and waved at her, gesturing that I had seen the staircase and I would take it.

I began climbing the stairs; it was so creepy. The spiral staircase was so tiny and narrow that nobody taller than a child could climb it comfortably. Finally, after much effort and some scratches on my arms, I reached the platform. I felt like a superhero. Shuchi had opened the door. Her eyes lit up when I handed her the cake. She couldn't believe what was happening and had an unforeseen spark in her eyes.

She called me in, but I refused and told her. "No, Shuchi. Not in an air-conditioned room, but in the breeze, under the sky. Let the stars and the scintillating moon become a witness of your birthday." I looked at her innocently; she seems touched that I remembered what she had told me.

"Happy birthday Shuchi. Wish you a world of happiness on this special day," I whispered and handed her the bouquet. "The most beautiful roses for the most beautiful girl in this world." Although she was wearing a simple night suit, she looked so stunning that I couldn't take my eyes off her. My heart was soothed on seeing her. I breathed the scent of her dress, her skin.

"Thank you, Sanjeev. So sweet! How did you manage to get this so late?" she said hugging the bouquet.

"I will tell you later dear. For now, I am going. If someone sees me here, they will beat me," I whispered. She giggled and it seemed my purpose of coming here was fulfilled.

"I know I am late…probably the last person to wish you."

"But this has been the best wish of the entire day. I will always remember this."

"I think I should leave now. I will call you after reaching home." She nodded and I hurriedly said, "Once again, happy birthday."

"Wait!" she said and opened the cake box then and there. She dug out a huge piece of the cake and asked me to open my mouth. She put the entire piece into my mouth; it was too big to fit in and I thought I'd choke. But then, she took back half of it and ate it herself. I don't know if I was imagining it, but that was the best cake I had ever tasted; her hands had touched it, after all.

"Now I am going. Bye," I said and started coming down the stairs.

"Go back carefully, Sanjeev," she said lovingly. "Let's meet tomorrow." She stood there till I reached down and went over the wall.

Seeing Ruchita nowhere, I got pissed. I dug out my phone and called her. "Where the hell are you? Did you just run away leaving me here?"

"No, stupid. Just look straight. I am right here, waving my hand." I saw Ruchita at a distance and rushed towards her.

"Why the hell did you move the car?" I asked, rubbing the dust off my pants.

"Because of the security guard. He asked me to park the car somewhere else. How did things go for you?" she asked.

"Thank you, Cupid!" I said and described what had happened and she laughed. Then a moment later, she made a serious face, and asked, "But where is my share of the cake?"

"Why are you asking me? It's not my birthday."

She had gotten it all worked out and now I had had the cake and met the birthday girl and she had been a mere driver.

"I don't get anything for driving you till here at this hour?" She made a puppy face saying this.

"Oh, drama queen!" I said, knowing well that she was pulling my leg. "No drama with me, okay. I know a bakery nearby that's open twenty-four hours. Let's go there and you can eat whatever you want." I said, strapping the seat belt. "My treat," I added.

She smiled and turned the key.

I called Shuchi after reaching the flat, but the call went unanswered. It was quite late anyway, as Ruchita and I had gone off for a small treat and ride after wishing Shuchi. This was the first time I had roamed on the roads so late in the night.

The next day, the three of us decided to meet up after college and my office. We met at a mall in Saket, and had a lot of fun. We cut a cake for Shuchi once again and celebrated the occasion we had missed. We were in the middle of munching on burgers when Ruchita's phone vibrated. She gulped down the big bite she had taken, and pulled the phone out of her jeans pocket. She said reading the message, "Guys, I shall leave now. Got some work. Dad is waiting for me. Will catch up with you guys soon."

She stood up, picked her bag up, ready to leave. But before she left, she came towards Shuchi, hugged her and said, "Happy birthday, sweetheart. Let's take a selfie with the birthday girl." She asked me to come over to their side. I got up from my chair to join them, and got ready to pose.

But I had a sense of uneasiness in posing and kept adjusting myself to get into the frame of the camera. Every time I raised my head to fit into the frame, I thought I looked weird. I had hardly been a part of any selfie before. Finally Ruchita clicked a selfie and gave her phone to us to look at. I looked the dumbest of all in the pic. I whispered, "As usual, I am looking like a zombie."

"Yes, absolutely." Ruchita chuckled.

"Uff, you don't. Ruchita, please stop teasing him," Shuchi came to my defence.

Ruchita laughed and said, "Okay, now I am going. You love birds carry on." She turned back and said, "Wait, I forgot to give you your birthday gift. This is for you." She dug out of her bag a small box packed in a beautiful packing paper with a ribbon on it. Shuchi thanked her and Ruchita left.

After that, we enjoyed our conversation for about an hour more. I asked her if she was getting late. She told me she had told aunty that she was with me and she had permission to be out till about eleven.

Since the mall was close to my flat, I asked Shuchi if she'd like to see where I lived. She was excited at the idea and agreed.

We took an auto and reached my flat. I entered and tidied up the place a bit, so she didn't feel uncomfortable. After all, she was coming to my place for the first time, and I was slightly nervous.

She took a seat on the chair, and watched me move around. I went to get her a glass of water and found her staring at me. I took a seat on the chair and looked at her. She was looking at me unblinkingly. I asked her, "What are you looking at?"

"Nothing, just your eyes. They reflect so many things."

"Like?"

She didn't say anything, instead came close to me. I remained seated and she stood bent over me, looking into my eyes.

I wondered, "*Why is she looking at me like that? So lovingly. I feel like looking at her with the same innocence, but I fear I'd end up saying something that I have wanted to for so long. Should I hold her? But what if she doesn't like it? She won't say anything till I do. I must take the first step. Oh, I am getting confused. I am such a loser. Shall I say something to change the topic? No, I should not. It might turn her off. I don't want to upset her. I like her. The space that was full of sadness once has has illuminated with her presence. Yes, with her, memories are receding in my mind but what if she is still struggling to put them behind her."*

Thinking thus, I gathered myself up to stand up and go to the makeshift kitchen to make coffee. But she held my shoulders and kissed me on the lips.

It was very sudden and unexpected. Before I could understand anything, I found myself kissing her provoking lips. I was lost in her, as if a world of happiness had opened up with her lips. When the spell broke and she took a step back, I felt that the broken pieces inside me were joining again to give life a new meaning.

I saw her; she was so close to me. I could feel her breath on my face. I sensed her coming closer and got the signal. I held her cheeks with both my hands and kissed her again, with unmatched fervor and a renewed passion. I knew she wanted it as much as me. We kissed for a while and then broke apart, only to breathe. My lips went lower, caressing her nape with light kisses and she moaned. That turned me on and I couldn't hold back any longer. My hands reached her waist and she reciprocated by making her kiss deeper and more sensuous. I could smell her perfume and that drove me wild. My hands slithered beneath her top and felt her soft skin. She moaned in my ear and murmured, "Sanjeev, I like you very much."

That broke the dam behind which I had been hiding my feelings. I held her tighter and closer. She was experiencing ecstasy like never before and dug her nails in my back, pulling me closer to her. I gently put my hands under her shirt and she moaned in pleasure. She was enjoying it, I could see, and was totally overwhelmed in love, just like me. I pulled off her shirt and was mesmerized with the beauty I saw. She quickly followed and pulled my t-shirt off. Her hands on my chest made me shiver with delight. An unseen force was knotting inside my chest, making me go wild with delight. One look at the hot red bra drove me off the edge and I hugged her tight, her hot flesh kindling the fire in my body. I started kissing her more passionately. I locked my hands behind her and tried to unhook her bra, to gain that intimacy that my heart had been craving for. But somehow, it got tangled and she started laughing.

"You are so stupid. You don't know how to unhook a girl's bra!" She laughed, and released me from her embrace. She unhooked it for me.

"How would I know? I haven't done it before. It was my first time." I hadn't wanted to say this. I felt embarrassed but seeing her smile, forgot all about it. In the meantime, I saw her removing her clothes.

We hugged again and kissed like two lovers driven crazy with love. We fell on the bed and explored each other's bodies with an unparalleled tenderness. The flame of passion, desire and love took control over us and consumed us. I wanted to feel her, all over. She moaned with pleasure; she had dreamt of this moment. But life had decided to make her dream come true. We crossed all barriers and became one, in mind, body and soul.

Moments of passion and ecstasy later, I lay by her side, panting and out of breath. I felt different, as if a part of me had revived. She lay on my chest, not saying a word.

"Shuchi, are you asleep?" I asked after sometime. She didn't respond, but she wasn't asleep. She opened her eyes, turned to me and looked at me with fond love. She kissed me on the cheek and lay her head on my chest again.

After a few moments of silence, she asked me, "Why is your heart beating so hard? I can almost hear it."

I didn't know what to tell her. That it was my first time and I was kind of nervous and feeling different. Something I had never felt before, and it was pretty emotional for me. Instead, I said, "You are very hot." She looked up and smiled. Both of us remained like that for some more time till someone rang the doorbell.

I thought it was the tiffin boy, but the doorbell rang again. We quickly straightened our clothes and I opened the door. It was Ruchita at the door.

"What a pleasant surprise, Ruchita. How come you're here?" I asked.

"Hi babes!" Shuchi also called out from behind me.

"You both look sleepy. Were you up to some hanky panky?" she said teasingly.

"No, no. Just talking. I was feeling sleepy so just got up to make some coffee," I said to cover up.

She didn't look convinced though, and Shuchi's blushing was only making me more nervous.

"I don't need coffee, love birds. I need to know what's cooking," she said and burst into laughter.

A sweet feeling swept over me when I looked at Shuchi. There was something so enthralling about her, that I had lost my heart to her.

True love is when you feel the other's pain as your own and fill their broken heart with your love, but a true relationship is when the other person also feels the same for you and fills up your broken heart with love. Something that you have longed for so many years. I started feeling the same for Shuchi. I hoped she felt the same for me.

The next day I had a crazy time at office, but the photography class was refreshing. Ruchita, as usual, kept giving me naughty smiles. I struggled to keep her off, but couldn't help smiling at the thought of Shuchi. Honestly, I wanted to spend some time with Ruchita too, lest she started feeling that I was ignoring her. In fact, this had been Shuchi's idea in the first place and I loved her more for it.

We were supposed to meet at the same mall in Saket the next evening after my office got over. The girls wanted to check out a new restro-bar cum club that had just opened up. Stags were not allowed in, so I had to anyway rely on them for getting in.

Ruchita was going crazy with the parking. "How the hell do they make this elevated parking thing work?" She had been trying to take the car forth, but the slope kept pulling her back. She seemed stuck, and was more furious because of the car that was honking from behind her. The guy driving it was continuously honking, perhaps scared that her car would roll back and bump into his expensive car.

He stopped honking and Ruchita heaved a sigh of relief. She saw him coming out of the car in her car's rear-view mirror. He walked towards her and asked, "Let me help you. I guess you are facing a problem in getting to the parking." Ruchita would have given him a piece of her mind for honking and making her nervous, but he had said it politely with a smile. It seemed like a helpful gesture rather than a condescending one.

"Yes, please. I don't understand what's wrong today. Trust me if you can, I drive pretty well. Today is just one unlucky day." She came out of the car and let the guy take the wheel.

The car was at such an angle on the upward curve that it took the guy a bit of effort to park it. As he came out and handed the keys to Ruchita, moments before rushing to get his own car, she thanked him and walked towards the mall.

"Where the hell are you? Don't tell me you haven't even started yet! Okay, but I have been waiting for so long now. Come quickly!" Ruchita shouted into the phone. She was standing right in front of Club Xplode, which we had decided to check out. She could hear wonderful music being played inside every time someone opened the door to go in. She wanted to go in too, but how would I get in then?

While she was waiting, a voice came from behind her, "Excuse me."

She turned around and saw the same guy who had helped her park the car. "Hey!"

"What a pleasant day for us! Met twice within half an hour." He beamed.

"Yes," she said with a smile.

"How come you're standing outside? Girls are allowed without a partner too, Madame." He laughed lightly on cracking the joke.

She also played along and said, "Oh my god! I wasted so much time waiting to enter."

He waved his hand to brush the topic aside and said, "I am sorry for the bad joke. I have just been dumped by my friends whose plan got cancelled all of a sudden." Ruchita made a face to show her sympathy, but then her face lit up with a smile when this chivalrous handsome boy said, "Can I join you? I saw you alone and wondered if your friends have also spoiled it for you."

"Oh my friend has definitely spoiled it, but he'll be here, no doubt. But please be my guest…join me till he is here! After that I am afraid…"

"Oh, no problem lady! I wouldn't want your boyfriend to think weird stuff about you because of me. You know…"

"Hey, hey!" Ruchita cut him short. "He isn't my boyfriend. So relax!"

"By the way, I am Rohan. And you?"

"Ruchita Narang."

They both went in and ordered their drinks – a Carlsberg Tuborg Strong for the guy and a Cosmopolitan for Ruchita.

When I reached the club almost forty-five minutes later, I couldn't see Ruchita anywhere, while I remembered clearly that she had said she was waiting at the entrance. I called her up and she told me she was inside. She came out in a couple of minutes and took me in; stags weren't allowed entry without a partner, after all. She guided me towards a table in the dim light of the club. By this time, I had begun grooving to the tune of the music playing. She pointed at a table and I gestured at her to walk ahead and take a seat. I was going to sit opposite her when I noticed someone sitting there already. Some guy I had never seen before. Might be her friend, I thought and took my seat next to Ruchita.

Ruchita took the role of the hostess automatically and said with a broad smile, "Sanjeev, meet Rohan! Rohan, this is Sanjeev."

We shook hands with each other. I looked at Ruchita and said, "You never told me about him, Ruchita. How mean! Since when has this been going on?" I asked curiously, happy that I finally had a chance to tease her too, and also a bit surprised that she hadn't told me about this guy ever before.

"I never told you because I didn't know him." Now that confused me quite a bit. She must have read my expression, so she explained, "Actually we just met. Like an hour back."

"What? I don't understand." Then Ruchita explained the entire episode to me.

I was baffled at how easily Ruchita had befriended a total stranger, but I didn't let it show. In the few minutes that we spent thereafter, I realized that Rohan seemed to have a good sense of humour. Moreover, Ruchita was laughing along with him at almost every other thing he said. His physique was proof that he was a regular at a gym. Spike gelled hair, fair skin, and a flirtiest way of talking – he could have been any girl's dream guy. It was evident through his speaking skills that he knew how to charm anyone, and could talk to anyone in any situation, unlike me. He was talking to Ruchita as if both were old friends meeting after a long time.

"So, what do you do, Rohan?" I asked sipping my drink. I didn't even know what it was, but it tasted good. Ruchita and Rohan had decided to order for me, as I was a novice.

"I am pursuing my MBA. Second year," he said.

"Oh, nice."

Just then, I received a call from Shuchi. She said she would reach in another fifteen minutes. Without much thought, I told her that we'd come out to receive her. After all, I was her knight in shining armour, I joked to Ruchita when she asked me why I had promised to go out.

In another ten minutes, we told Rohan that we had to leave, as the princess was going to arrive anytime now. He bade us goodbye without much ado. We cleared the bill and came out, while Rohan said goodbye and went the other way.

I had a full-fledged chance to tease Ruchita now. "So, you like this guy, *haan*?"

"Why would you say that? We just met. He is okay, but not my type." She had managed to puncture my spirit in just one go. Suddenly my phone buzzed.

It was a call from Shuchi and I thought she'd have reached the place and was calling to ask where we were. But she informed us that she was heading back home as her mother had hurt herself in the kitchen and needed her help. I asked her if she needed me, and she promised to let me know the situation as soon as she reached home. So Ruchita and I also decided to head back home and meet again soon.

An accident happened while another accident awaited for Shuchi. Her mom being hurt may have delayed the upcoming accident.

Ruchita told me later that she and Rohan had become friends and had gone out once.

One evening, when Ruchita was watching TV, her phone vibrated. It was Rohan.

Hey. Wassup. Long time. How you doing? Seems these days you are able to park the car successfully. ;)

Ruchita: *Hey. Haha. Not really. I still need help. :D*

Rohan: *Busy these days?*

Ruchita: *Kind of. You tell me.*

Rohan: *Where are you now?*

Ruchita: *At home. Chilling after a long day. In my shorts. ;)*

Rohan: *Hot. But I won't believe it until I see you in shorts. ;)*

Ruchita: *So you want proof. Why don't you come home? I am all alone.*

Rohan: *Someone is so desperate. Coming in some time. :P*

He reached Ruchita's home in fifteen minutes as he didn't want to waste a single minute.

"Today is the day for some hanky panky," he whispered to himself and a mischievous smile came onto his face. Just before pressing the doorbell, he took a deep breath, exhaled his breath onto his palm and smelled it. "Good enough," he said to himself.

Ruchita opened the door, as expected.

"Hey Ruchita, you asked me to come, and here I am," he flirted the moment he entered the room.

"Yes, I can see that. You are too quick." Both of them came into the drawing room.

"Wow. It's so huge and beautiful," he looked around the room and said.

"So… Why were you so adamant on coming home?" she asked and sat beside him on the sofa.

"What could be a more beautiful reason than to know that a beautiful girl is at home, alone?" He winked wickedly.

"Oh, that's good."

"No, actually it has been quite a few days since we met. You were occupied with your college, so I thought I'd come home and meet you. Even though we met once outside, but that was for a very short period of time. So when you told me that no one is at home for some time, I thought we can spend some quality time together."

"Yes, it's been a long time. Even I had been thinking of calling you, but somehow couldn't get time. So what are we going to do now?"

"Romance would be a good idea," he flirted.

"Very funny. Wait, I'll bring coffee for you."

"Yes, that's the second good idea after what I suggested. But for you, I can switch its priority number."

"Don't think too much. Coffee is the only good idea for now."

"Yes, coffee flavored condoms! Brilliant idea. That's what I am also saying."

"You are really one-track minded. I am talking about coffee, the beverage." And saying that, she went into the kitchen.

A few minutes later, Rohan walked behind her to the kitchen and held her from behind.

"Rohan, what are you doing?"

"Just came to see how you look while making coffee for me?"

"Oh really?" She didn't make any attempts to resist.

"Yes. See, the coffee looks so hot…," saying this, he kissed her neck and whispered in her ears, "Just like you. Driving me crazy."

"Enough, Rohan. It's too much now," Ruchita said without giving much air to him.

His hands were caressing her back slowly. The smoothness of her skin and the scent of her hair drove him crazy. He kept kissing her neck and letting her fragrance work its magic.

"You smell so good. It's getting on my mind, baby," he said.

"Okay! Enough. The coffee is ready. Let's go and sit outside." Ruchita was about to pick up both the coffee mugs when Rohan saw Ruchita biting her lowerlip, perhaps to curb her temptation. He knew this was the perfect time.

"Coffee can wait baby, but not me." With that, he lifted her up. Since she did not have the tiniest idea that he would lift her up, she cried out in horror. "What are you doing? I might just fall!"

"Do you think my well-toned biceps would let you slip out?" He grinned. And when Ruchita smiled too, he got the signal.

He brought her to the sofa and gently placed her, placing himself right on top. He started caressing her body, feeling the curves and touching every inch of her. Within seconds, he pulled her towards him and locked his lips with hers. Dexterously, he removed her t-shirt and let his hands feel her soft flesh.

"You are so sexy, Ruchita," he said, bringing his mouth close to her naval and kissing it. Ruchita moaned in pleasure as her hands caressed his hair, egging him on.

"Don't you think you will look sexier without these clothes?" he said, looking at her hungrily.

"Here? On the sofa?" Ruchita asked, her eyes still closed.

"Why waste time, baby? Plus, the bedroom is too clichéd. Sofa is sexy. Let me show you how much."

"But you remove your t-shirt first," she said teasingly. "Let me feel that muscular body." She opened her eyes to look at him, desire overtaking her senses. He wouldn't want anything else and removed the t-shirt quickly.

Rohan said, "Now it's your turn. Let me do it for you baby." He took his hands behind her back to unhook her bra, to set her assets free. His mouth was hungrily devouring hers as he tried to unhook it.

Ruchita pulled back and asked, "What are you looking for?"

It was kind of embarrassing for him to ask where the hooks were. She smiled mischievously and said, "Ever heard of a sports bra? Sometimes, my dear," she pulled his cheeks, "there are no hooks." She started laughing at his stupidity. She removed it for him. He moved towards her bottom and started sliding down the shorts she was wearing and before he could tongue her, they were startled with the doorbell ringing.

"What the fuck!" he whispered angrily at the lost opportunity.

Ruchita hurriedly scooped up her top from the floor and pulled it on. She used her nails to straighten her hair and asked Rohan to sit quietly on the sofa.

She opened the door and saw her dad.

"Dad, you are early today!" She smiled.

"Yes, the court was adjourned early today." He entered and saw Rohan.

"Who is this gentleman?"

"Dad, meet Rohan. My friend."

He stood up and both shook hands with each other. "Beta, I am just going to collect some files from my office. Rohan, don't forget the coffee before you leave," he said and left as swiftly as he had come.

"Ruchita, let's continue where we had left," Rohan tried to coax her into their little love game again.

"No, not today. Dad is home. If he sees you close to me, trust me, he will file a rape case against you." And she laughed seeing Rohan's poker face.

"Okay, let me bring the coffee for you. At least this much I can do for you to lift your mood." She smiled and left for the kitchen.

While sipping coffee, Ruchita asked, "So what's your plan for this weekend?"

"Haven't thought of anything yet. Why?"

"Actually it's my birthday tomorrow, so I am planning to throw a party this weekend. Would love it if you can join me. There will be other friends as well."

"Oh you never told me it's your birthday tomorrow otherwise I would have planned something for us, baby," he said lovingly. "I will definitely come."

"Okay, done. I will text you the venue when it's decided."

The Saturday evening that followed, I finished my work quickly, went back to the room, freshened up and changed into more suitable clothes and left for the birthday party that Ruchita had planned for her close friends in Club Xplode. After all, we had been unable to check it out the last time. This time we thought to enjoy the party of Shuchi and Ruchita together.

Out of habit, I reached the pub much before time. Ruchita messaged that she would reach a bit late as she was stuck in traffic. I called up Shuchi to check where she was, but her phone was not reachable. I tried several times, but it was of no use. I started roaming about and crossed the club entrance several times. One of those numerous times when I crossed the club entrance, the door swung open fiercely and I turned around to see the source of the sudden noise. A girl had just stormed out of the club. She wasn't able to walk properly, perhaps was swinging under the influence of alcohol. She had even taken her stilettoes in her hand and was now walking bare-feet. It intrigued me. She walked a little further away from the club, sat down on the staircase. She looked exhausted, and her cheeks were smeared with her kohl and mascara. She lowered her head in her lap and started crying. A few moments later, a guy came out looking for someone. He walked towards her and tried to console her. I was glued to the spot, looking at them, curious to know what would have made the girl be so sad.

The boy was trying hard to console her, but to no avail. When he tried to lift her head up, she became angry and a heated argument followed. I couldn't hear what was being said, but the volume and body language convinced me that it wasn't something very pleasant. The guy started shouting at her at the highest volume possible and I could see the contortions on his face. Sensing some trouble brewing, one bouncer rushed towards them and tried to settle the dispute. The girl left the place, crying and holding the stilettoes in her hand. I felt sad for her, and spontaneously rushed towards the railings to see where she was going. I couldn't find her anywhere, but saw Ruchita walking into the mall. Within minutes, she reached me. She was wearing a royal blue dress and was looking very different. Stilettoes. Hot red lipstick. A hint of make-up on her face. I had seen this side of her for the first time, and she knew very well how to carry herself. I was stunned.

"You can close your mouth, you know. It's open big enough to fit in two *golgappas*," she remarked coming closer to me.

"What the fuck…" I was about to ask her what had she done to herself that she looked so amazing, but she cut me short.

"What the fuck…how can I look so hot?" she said coquettishly. "Is that what you wanted to ask?"

Ruchita had always left me speechless with her uncanny prowess to read my mind, but just to tease her, I said, "No, I was not saying that. In fact, I was going to ask something else. Even with such a nice dress and lip colour, how can someone look so ugly?"

She frowned at me, and her eyebrows almost touched each other, her nose cringing in anger. She rubbed her hands together and asked, "What do you want? A slap or my stilettoes on your head?"

"Oh! So you're not open to criticism, I guess. Only praise, you narcissist girl!" I winked. She mock frowned again and I couldn't hold my laughter for any longer. It came out spontaneously and made Ruchita smile.

"Okay okay," I said raising my hands up in the air, "You were right. I was about to say what you guessed so accurately. You are looking extremely ravishing today. Since I haven't seen you like this before, I was stunned." I said, looking straight into her eyes. And this made her smile. Taking the cue, I continued, "See, here is your smile. The most precious jewel that can ever wear. I can make a million dollars if I describe it in my author style!" I said lovingly, stretching my hand to pull her cheek, like someone would do to a child.

"Oh really! A million dollars, I see!" Her lips widened into a scintillating smile. "Let's hear what the author has to say."

I shuffled the hair at the back of my head and thought hard about how this could be made more fun. Ruchita had been quietly listening to me and raised her eyebrows to tell me to start off. "Okay, let me think," I said to buy some more time, but she was continuously staring at me.

I finally decided to tease her; I would have a hundred chances to make up for it tonight. "Ruchita, you look beautiful. Your eyes are so black that even coal would feel shy looking at them." I could see her smile diminish a bit, but I continued nonetheless. "Your lips, though smeared with a lipstick that reminds me of blood, look like a ripe pomegranate." By now, her smile had completely gone and I was sure she was wondering if I was praising her or making fun of her. "Black silky hair falling on the nape and caressing your back…like the roots of a banyan tree falling all over…" Before I could complete, I turned to one side and saw Shuchi frowning at me. Ruchita burst into laughter.

Oh gosh! Have I overplayed the prank? I hope she doesn't think Ruchita and I had preplanned this about her. If I say something in my defence, Shuchi will be sure that we are the culprits. Moreover, she could very well think that I had been flirting with Ruchita. What will I do if that happens! Oh god!

"What's going on?" Shuchi asked, looking at me and then at Ruchita. Her face was bereft of any excitement to party now.

"Nothing is happening, my dear. He was just flirting with me." That would be the last nail on the coffin, I thought. She did what I had been fearing.

I protested immediately. "No, that's not true."

"What a liar! He did it purposely, trust me," Ruchita said holding Shuchi by her arm.

"I did it knowingly, yes, but she didn't have a clue about it. I just made it up right now to tease her a bit, dear." I really wanted to change the way this conversation was going. I hinted at Ruchita to change the topic, but looking at her mischievous smile I was sure she was enjoying the show.

Shuchi rolled her eyes and anger seemed to be the only emotion visible on her face.

"Are we here to fight or are we planning to go inside the club?" I attempted to change the topic.

"Don't change the topic," Shuchi said, catching me yet again. I wondered how she knew my mind and heart so well.

Ruchita chuckled and said, "Shuchi, spare him! Poor guy was only trying to act smart and we have teased him enough." With that, both of them high-fived and started laughing out loud.

"So it was your plan to upset me," I said, not believing that they had managed to fool me. I put my hands on my waist, looking at both of them accusingly.

Shuchi put her arm through mine and pulled me towards the club. "Shall we go in now, or are we waiting for someone else?" She had a twinkle in her eyes and I couldn't have been angry with her after that.

By the time we reached the entrance door, we saw a small queue of entrants. At the end of the line, right outside the club door, I could see a guy in a black suit noting down the names and contact number of the visitors and putting a stamp on the back of their hand before letting them in. *Must be a way to recognize people who had gained rightful entry into the club, I thought.*

When we entered through the multicoloured door, I was unable to see anything. It was so dark inside as compared to the brightly lit corridor outside. Nice music was on full blast and people were dancing next to their tables also, without any inhibitions. The dance floor was also full of people, some of them dancing crazy steps.

On the other side of the dance floor, there were tables where many couples and groups were seated, sipping their drinks. The ambience looked quite energetic. Almost everyone around me was dressed in their best; handsome men and gorgeous women wherever the gaze went. I became conscious again because I was dressed in casuals.

You can't go back into that world of depressive thoughts and loneliness. This life is so beautiful; you are enjoying with them. Don't think about your uneasiness and enjoy these moments, my mind told me and I decided to go with the flow.

Meandering between the crowds, we finally made our way to the bar counter. In fact, I just followed Ruchita and Shuchi. There was an empty table next to the counter, but there were only two chairs around it. Ruchita and Shuchi happily took the seats and I was left standing. Looking at my confused expression, Ruchita must have guessed I was feeling conscious and uneasy, so she got up and went up to the next table which had a vacant chair. She asked the couple if she could take the spare chair and got it back to our table in less than a minute.

In between our conversation, Ruchita seemed glued to her phone. I asked her if it was something urgent, and she waved it off saying it was some friend we didn't know.

I had begun to settle down when Ruchita announced. "I will have vodka with cranberry juice." I nodded and looked at Shuchi.

She thought for a moment and said, "I think I will have Sex on the Beach." My eyes flew wide open and I looked at her surprised, almost horrified.

She smiled and put her hand on mine on the table, saying, "It's the name of a drink that they make with vodka, peach, cranberry and orange juices."

They both now turned to me and I said defencively, "I will just have a fruit punch, I guess." I didn't know what to order and didn't have much knowledge when it came to alcohol as well. I was a novice.

"Sanjeev, aren't you having any hard drink?" Ruchita asked.

"I will…just want to start slow," I said and they both smiled at my nervousness.

"You can have beer, Sanjeev. It doesn't make you high if you drink slowly. And draught beer won't taste too bad too. What say?" Ruchita asked. I looked at Shuchi and she nodded lovingly, so I also nodded.

Ruchita went up to the bar counter and ordered our drinks. So I found out that it was self-service. After the first round of drinks, when the DJ played some party music, Ruchita stepped down from the seat and said, "Let's dance. Rocking music!"

I hesitated, but she pulled me towards the dance floor. We all danced for a few minutes and came back to our table sweating.

"Hey, let's have tequila shots. It will be fun," Shuchi suggested. By that time, I had also started enjoying the ambience and wanted to enjoy myself. So I didn't resist.

The beer had tasted awful to begin with, not to forget its smell, but it did seem nice after a few sips.

The bartender handed us three tequila shots with a slice of lemon each and some salt on the rim of the glass.

I was a bit scared at first, staring at the glass as if it had poison.

I was jolted out of my thoughts by Ruchita's voice. "On the count of three." Shuchi looked excited, so I forced a smile too.

"One…Two…Three!"

We all took up the glass, gulped down the tequila in one shot, licked the salt around the periphery and squeezed the lemon in our mouths. It tasted so bitter to me at first, then salty and then tangy. I wanted to puke it.

I looked at Shuchi. It seemed she was enjoying it a lot and was completely engrossed in it. Ruchita was fidgeting with her mobile phone again.

They ordered a repeat, but I declined.

"Sanjeev, one more shot, come on!" Ruchita requested.

"No, one was enough for me."

"Don't spoil the party, Sanjeev," Ruchita said. "Shuchi, you tell him."

"Sanjeev, for me. One more shot," Shuchi said sweetly, and I couldn't refuse.

And we did it again. Ruchita started shouting and pulled us towards the dance floor again. It was a crazy night. After about five minutes, I started feeling dizzy. I left the dance floor and came back to the table. I saw Shuchi following me, and Ruchita joining us soon after. We all took our seats, looked at each other, and started laughing without any reason. I was drunk. And happy.

"Hey, Ruchita!" someone called out aloud over the din of the loud music from behind us.

We all turned back to see who it was. Rohan Awasthi. The same guy that Ruchita and I had met the other day.

Ruchita smiled broadly and said, "Hey! Nice to see you again." Saying that, Ruchita hugged him.

So this was what the messaging had been about; Ruchita was interested in this guy! And why not! He was good looking, looked polished and well-mannered too. I was happy for Ruchita.

When I turned to Shuchi to explain who this guy was, my face froze. She sat there completely motionless. As if the impact of the tequila had vanished completely. As if she had seen a ghost.

Before I could say a single syllable, she shouted hoarsely, "What the hell are you doing here?" Her face was bereft of any emotions, barring pain.

"Oh my god, Shuchi. You are also here. What a pleasant surprise!" he said in a very pleasing tone and tried keeping his hands on her shoulders to hug her. I could guess where this was leading, and prayed to every god who could hear me over the loud music of the nightclub that I be proved wrong.

"Take your hands off me! Don't you dare!" Shuchi said in a very cold tone.

"Why are you here?" she asked again. I looked at Ruchita; she had no clue what was happening.

Shuchi's rudeness finally started getting onto Rohan's nerves. Throwing off his mask of being polite and pleasing, he said, "Listen, even I can raise my voice. So calm down. Ruchita invited me here, and I had no fucking clue you were coming." Shuchi's face went pale as she looked at Ruchita and back at Rohan.

"If I had a clue that a swine like you would be coming here, I wouldn't have come in the first place." Shuchi was really pissed seeing him. She turned towards Ruchita and asked in the same angry tone, "How do you know him?"

Sensing the situation getting out of control and sure there was something to it that she wasn't aware of, Ruchita replied calmly, "We just met a few days ago and have been chatting up. Nothing more than that...But what happened, Shuchi? Why are you so upset?"

"So, he didn't tell you anything? Oh, wait! That's not his strategy, you see! He will be nice to you till he sleeps with you and then will show his true colours."

Ruchita was stunned. She looked at me and then at Rohan, wondering what was happening.

Shuchi seemed to be holding her emotions in check when she said, "He is my ex."

I had managed to guess it but Ruchita looked shell shocked. She covered her mouth with her hand, realizing the impact of what had just happened.

"Enough Shuchi! Look, whatever happened has happened. It's the past. And it was between us. There is no need to say such nasty things about me to others. I am sure there's some misunderstanding," he said, and tried to keep his hand on her shoulder once again.

"Misunderstanding? You bastard! You ruined my life. You befriended me so that you could beguile me with your looks and charming words. Only so that you could sleep with me, and when I didn't agree to it, you forced me. Not just that, when I tried to run away, you slapped me. You little piece of shit! It's because of you that I had forgotten to live life. Because of you, I couldn't trust anyone again. Because of you, my life became miserable and I wanted to quit everything. Because of the pain and fear you created in me in the name of a relationship!" Shuchi was hysterical and I had to step forward and hold her lest she collapsed. I knew she had been affected by what Rohan did, but not to this extent! I wanted to beat the shit out of this guy who had hurt my Shuchi, but holding her and being with her was far more important.

She was almost on the verge of crying, but she held it back. I had never seen her like this before. She was speaking her heart out.

"You bastard! Just stay away from me and don't ever show me your face," she continued.

Then there came a moment when everyone fell silent. The kind of silence that is usually the harbinger of something horrible.

"Darling, forget it! I told you it was the past. Come on, cheer up! And let's dance," Rohan said shamelessly and held Shuchi's hand again.

I couldn't believe how shameless he was! Ruchita had been a mute spectator till now, because she knew she had done something wrong, without intending to. But now, she held Rohan's hand and said, "Just leave her alone, Rohan."

A few people turned around hearing the heated argument.

It was time for me to interfere, I sensed, as Shuchi had gained some confidence with Ruchita's interference. That too against Rohan.

But just then, Rohan spoke up again. "See, I have moved on. You seem to have moved on too. Is he your new boyfriend?" he said, pointing at me.

I got so furious at his shamelessness that I came forward and said firmly, "Dude, just go away and this will end peacefully."

"Hey, I wasn't talking to you. Just stay where you belong," he said and pushed me towards the counter.

That was it! I gestured at Ruchita to take care of Shuchi and stepped forward. Before he could anticipate what I was up to, I had punched him on his face. He wasn't prepared for this blow and fell down. It was the first time I had punched someone. I knew I wasn't strong enough to fight it out with him – especially after I had seen his well-toned body – but whatever was happening in front of my eyes had already gone out of control.

He stood up and punched me back. The blow was so heavy that I fell down and sensed something trickling down my nose. Blood, I presumed. I had never felt such a blow before this and was shaken. Before something more could happen, two bouncers came and asked us to stop the fight. We struggled to get back at each other, but they clutched our hands and took us outside the club. Rather threw us out. The DJ had already stopped playing the music and almost everyone present was looking at us.

Ruchita and Shuchi followed me. Shuchi was still on the verge of crying. An air of stern, deep, and irredeemable gloom hung over the place. Rohan left immediately thereafter, knowing well that Ruchita would not give him more attention. And Ruchita was caught amid all the mess without any fault of hers.

Without saying anything to anyone, Shuchi fidgeted with her phone. I went close to her and tried to hold her in my arms.

She said, "I have called a cab to take me home. Will catch you later."

I tried to stop her but Ruchita asked me to let her be. So I just asked Shuchi to drop a message when she reached home before she left.

It all fell silent again.

"It wasn't my mistake," Ruchita said helplessly.

"I know," I said holding her hand and consoling her.

One incident can change everything. Especially if it's about the past. It takes months and months, sometimes more than a year to move on, but one silly incident can take you back to the past and will remind you of everything again. The same happened with Shuchi. As she lay on her bed that night, her thoughts went back to that fateful night.

A fresher's party had been organized by the seniors after a month of initial ragging and elections for the various student council posts. Everyone was invited and first year students like her were super excited. After all, it was going to be the first party that they'd be attending together in a pub near the college. Shuchi reached the venue in her new red one-piece dress that she had bought for this party specially. She wore matching jewellery and the perfect high heels with it.

The moment she opened the thick doors and stepped in, music at its highest possible volume hit her eardrums. The dance floor was overflowing as students danced energetically. Drinks were being served on one side of the dance floor, while on the opposite side, dinner was being laid out. Shuchi was pretty excited tonight; she had decided to drink with her friends as they were planning to spend the night at a classmate's PG, with no fear of reaching home drunk.

She joined her gang of friends who were having tequila shots. She also started off and had four shots before she realized that it was getting too much. This was her first tryst with alcohol and it had started showing its impact on her mind. She turned around toward the main gate to get some fresh air. She was about to trip, thanks to her high heels, but slammed right into Rohan Awasthi – the president of the student council and a final year student. He held her perfectly, as if he knew that it was going to happen and had been waiting for the moment.

"Relax, Shuchi," he said, holding her. She looked at him. His eyes were large and he had a mischievous smile on his face. She noticed that he was good looking, but his looks were accentuated even more when he smiled like that; the dimples on his cheeks made him look like a charming prince. Rohan supported her body that seemed to be out of her control at that moment, and made her walk slowly towards the exit. Some fresh air would help her, he reasoned. So they went near the garden and he made her sit in a corner.

They had met several times in college after the first day when Rohan's group had ragged them playfully. They used to meet before classes, after classes and even during some classes when they were bunking. With him, every day was like a party and the first time he kissed her was just out of this world. It was near the library in the evening, when nobody was around, just before they headed for this party. Not many of Shuchi's friends knew about this.

He had fixed the library as the meeting place. When Shuchi reached there, he took her hand and pulled her in the corner. It was as silent as a graveyard. Rain pattered on the window at the end of the corridor where they stood, and for her, it was perfectly romantic. Just a glimpse of her in that dress had made Rohan melt. He leaned in closer to her and ended up kissing her. He knew how to kiss a girl, and she was feeling sensations she had never felt. But a minute later, when they heard some sound, he pulled away. She looked at him, the glint in his eyes matching with her shy, yet scintillating smile.

The smile became wider when she saw the smear of her lipstick on his mouth. Shuchi extended a hand to clean it up, but Rohan pulled himself away and said jocularly, "Again?Are you sure?" and winked at her.

She was taken aback at his naughtiness and almost shouted, "No, you duffer. There's lipstick on your lips. You destroyed my MAC."

"Oh really?" he said and Shuchi nodded lovingly. "Then let me keep your costly MAC on my lips as a memento of this special moment."

Her smile at this was shy and scintillating. She wished she could capture this moment somewhere, but it was definitely captured in her mind. For a girl, the first kiss is always memorable, and so was it for Shuchi.

Rohan had a different way of remembering it. He wrote a note describing the first kiss and their intimate meetings on Facebook, tagging her in the post.

When she saw a whole lot of notifications on her Facebook account, she wondered what the post was about. On seeing the note, she was anything but happy. Very upset.

"Why would you do that? Please delete it right away," Shuchi told Rohan.

"But why baby? Isn't it romantic? I wrote it myself; in fact, stayed up the entire night to complete it." Rohan sounded disappointed.

"It's good. Very good, if you ask me. But please untag me. I don't want people to keep visiting my profile to stalk me."

"Okay, I will do that. Please don't get upset."

"Thanks."

He untagged Shuchi. The write up was definitely a pretty romantic description of whatever happened that night, and their several subsequent meetings in the last two weeks. But it was quite strange. Shuchi could only recall half the things that he had written about the night of the party. She re-read the note several times but it still felt strange.

A message popped up on her Facebook messenger just then.

'Hey! Are you there? If you don't want to type, I can come up and talk to you in person. Generally girls don't like to type much... until it's is her boyfriend chatting.' Rohan pinged.

The last line caught her attention.

'How many girls are you chatting up with simultaneously that you know such small details about girls?'

'Nothing like that yaar. Just that one girl who happened to be the general secretary always preferred calls, and she had once mentioned this.'

'Okay.' Shuchi replied curtly.

A few moments later, he pinged again. 'You didn't say anything?'

'About what?'

'About me coming over to your place?'

'Now?' Shuchi was not sure.

'Yes, of course. Why would I plan for two years down the line?'

'Isn't it too late for that?'

Shuchi's phone was ringing; it brought her out of her thoughts when her mom called her. She was in the balcony, lost in her thoughts.

It was around 10 p.m. and her mom was watching a news channel on TV. She picked up the phone and passed it on to Shuchi.

"Ruchita's call for you," she said. It was Ruchita's fourth call.

Shuchi didn't look too excited about it. Her mom sensed her uneasiness and gestured at her to take the call and left her alone in the room.

"Hey, Shuchi," said Ruchita, a little hesitant after whatever had happened at the club.

"Hi," Shuchi replied out of courtesy.

"I know whatever happened at the club has hurt you badly, but I swear to god I didn't even have a tiny clue about that idiot. In fact, I have never seen him in college also. I didn't even know the whole story. He had told me that he had graduated from the same university, but it never occurred to me that he'd be from the same college, and moreover that he'd be such a loser. I am really sorry that I hurt you," Ruchita said in one go, without even taking a breath in between.

Shuchi remained silent; she understood that Ruchita was not to be blamed. She knew her friends would never hurt her on purpose.

"Please say something. I am really sorry for this fiasco. I didn't mean to hurt you Shuchi. I wasn't aware of anything. From now onwards, I will kick that guy if I see him ever…or maybe just slap him hard."

It took several seconds before Shuchi spoke, "I understand, Ruchita. I didn't know this about him when I met him too. He is such a swine."

"I know now. After listening to you last night when you were shouting at him, I realized and was able to connect the dots that how sweetly he was trying to woo me. Tried flirting with me."

"Yes, that's his signature style to trap girls."

"You know Shuchi, sometimes I think the same thing happened with me as well. The guy was such a creep and he was with me for the same reason. I feel guys who are notorious, who just try to appear like nice guys so they can seduce girls, play with our feelings very easily. And because they are showing off so much love, girls like us also fall for them. And in all this confusion, when we bump into really nice guys, who care for us genuinely, but are unable to show off their love like the other losers, they either get friend-zoned or we just stop talking to them. Later, when things go wrong with us, we just say all guys are the same. We are hardwired like this."

"You are right. My mom says the same thing to me."

"So are we good?"

"Absolutely. We are. BFF!" Shuchi smiled after a long time.

"Thank you. I thought you'd never even take my call. But Sanjeev encouraged me to talk to you. Isn't he sweet?"

"Yes, he is. He knows how I feel even before I know it myself," Shuchi said and blushed.

"Ooh, so the story has reached till here," Ruchita quipped. "I know how nice he is, that's why I have made him Dr Watson." Ruchita laughed.

Shuchi also joined her and said, "Yes, he told me about it. And you are Lady Sherlock."

"I would prefer Mrs Holmes. The guy who plays Sherlock in the Holmes series on TV is so hot," Ruchita said dreamily and both of them broke into laughter.

Since I had been unable to give Shuchi her gift on her birthday, I had promised myself to do something special for her. And now, I had two gifts pending – one for Ruchita as well. That night at the pub, I had to carry it back with me because things had come up unexpectedly. The gift that Shuchi had got for Ruchita was also with me because she had left it at the club the other day. So I thought I'd use it as a reason to meet her.

It had been a few days after the club incident, and although Shuchi was okay talking to me and Ruchita over phone, she refused to come out and meet either of us. So I thought of visiting her. So one fine evening after office, I directly went to her house. After ringing the doorbell a few times, her mom opened the door.

"Sanjeev! It's so nice to see you," she beamed. "Please come inside."

I greeted her, came inside and sat on the couch.

"Actually, aunty, two back days, Shuchi had brought this gift for Ruchita. But after the incident, I am sure you are aware of it, she forgot it there. So I've just come to give it to her," I said, taking out the gift from my bag.

"It's good that you came here." She took the gift and kept it on the other side of the table.

"Is Shuchi home? I can't see her," I asked.

"No, she has just gone out for some work. Must have left some twenty minutes back. She must be on her way back. Let me call her," she said. "Would you like to have something?"

"No, aunty. Thanks," I said and judging her mood, I continued, "Aunty, actually I was thinking that after that incident, Shuchi is hurt, although it wasn't Ruchita's fault. Even though she has been talking to us, her mood is still upset and she doesn't feel joyous about anything. "

"Yes, I can see that she is still upset, but I am sure she will be fine soon. Memories always haunt one."

"You're right. So I was thinking of taking her on a trip. A whole day trip, if you give permission," I asked cautiously.

"A trip? Where?" I suddenly had all her attention.

"I haven't thought it out yet, but somewhere nearby. She'll feel good."

"Who else is coming with you?" she enquired.

"Ruchita will join us later in the day. I will inform you about the location where we are going."

"And why are you asking for permission? You could have lied about it and taken her on this trip."

"Well, Shuchi had told me she generally spends the weekends with you. With her college and your job, weekends are the only time you get. So she always says, 'weekends are for my mom'. And since this trip will be on a Sunday, I wanted to take permission for intrusion into your time with your daughter."

She thought for a moment and smiled, "I am glad that you are so thoughtful. Yes, we spend time together on weekends, but it's fine with me if she goes out with you guys. I am sure you will take care of her. Just don't be late while coming back. I am sure she will be very happy."

"Yes, I hope so."

When Shuchi didn't turn up for the next twenty minutes too, and did not even take aunty's calls, I finally took my leave.

I called up Ruchita a night before the trip that I had planned for Shuchi. She didn't pick up the call. After an hour, she called me back.

"What's up, Dr Watson? Is there any new case on your blog?" she said excitedly.

"No, no case. People understand that you are of no use these days. Mrs Holmes is totally useless. Always into food," I teased her on similar lines.

"Waah! Sense of humour. Good, good." We both laughed.

"Listen, you were telling me that day that I should plan something for her to make her feel special. I listened to your advice," I said.

"Great. So what's the plan?"

"I am taking her out for the whole day. There are a few things I have planned for her. Actually after that incident, I know she was hurt. Though it was nobody's fault, she has been sad ever since. So I thought of planning this trip," I said. "Honestly, I haven't asked her out. I went to meet her at her home, but she wasn't there. But I took her mom's permission, and she agreed. Hope Shuchi agrees too."

"Wow. That's really sweet. See, I told you, she likes you too or maybe she loves you too. She will agree. Don't worry. By the way, when are you leaving? And where do you plan to take her?"

"This weekend. The plan is to take her to Damdama Lake. It's a two-hour drive from here. I have planned a few more things for the day."

"Oh, so finally the romantic author in you is coming out. Do you want to take my car?"

"No, thanks. I have talked to one agency. They have said that they can give me a car on rent for the whole day. They will drop the car to my place tomorrow morning. I will pick up Shuchi and then head for the lake."

"So everything is planned out. I am the last person to know about this secret plan. Seriously, I am failing as Mrs Holmes. I should have observed it before your telling me."

"Enough of your drama. Listen, I lied to her mom about a small thing. I told her that you will be joining us later."

"Why would you do that?"

"Her mom was adamant in knowing who else is coming for the trip. So I had to take your name. But in case she calls you, you just make some excuse."

"Okay, Dr Watson. Anything for you. Enjoy and tell me everything once you guys are back."

When I met her on Saturday evening, I asked her to be available the next day because I had a surprise for her. I had finally planned the trip for both of us – a special day. I was quite excited about the trip and ensured I did not tell Shuchi where we were going. It had to be a surprise for her. I had never surprised anyone before this, and in fact, whenever I had planned to, I had not been able to hide it for long. They would request to know, and I would tell them to see their smile. But this time I wanted to be extra careful and keep mum, and make my surprise trip successful. She even asked me when I went to drop her till the main gate, but I resisted the temptation.

"Sanjeev, where are we going? Tell me na! What do you have in mind, I am very curious." She looked so happy at just the prospect of a surprise, I was wondering what would happen when she actually found out. That feeling gave me a kick.

"You will come to know tomorrow. It's just a matter of twelve hours." I winked.

"At least tell me who else is going apart from us?" She hadn't given up yet.

"Tomorrow. You will come to know everything tomorrow. Just wait and see. You don't have any other option." I smiled and left for my apartment.

The next morning, I woke up early. I had already packed my bag with the essentials. I called up the travel agent and asked him to send the car to my apartment in an hour. It was a Hyundai Verna, a classy sedan which had been my favourite for long. I had rented the car, which I was to drive. I had already paid the agent the rent in advance for the car, which was to be sent back to him before 10 p.m.

In about forty-five minutes, my doorbell rang and a man dressed in white handed over the keys of the car. He took my signature on a form and went away. I called up Shuchi and asked her to be ready in half an hour, but she said she was already geared up for the day. I drove towards her house and upon reaching, called her. Within minutes, she came out dressed like an angel. Her mother followed her till the gate. She waved at me and I did the same. We also exchanged an assuring smile through which I promised I'd take care of Shuchi.

While I was looking at her mother, her surprise on seeing the car didn't escape me. Shuchi gave me a bemused smile.

"Come, hurry," I said and she hopped in.

Once we were out of her territory, she again asked, "I think now you can tell me where we are going? You can end the suspense?"

"Nope. Not yet. You will see where we are going. If I tell you, you will start Googling it and then I won't have anything to show you."

"No, I won't Google. Promise!" She kept her phone in the dashboard and said, "See, you can keep my phone, but at least tell me now."

I was amused at her dramatic dialogues, but still retained my stance. "No."

"Okay, who else is going?"

"Well, I can tell you that." She smiled that broad smile of hers that drives me crazy. "Apart from the both of us, Ruchita might join us later."

"Okay."

"You just enjoy the long drive. I know you love them." I smiled and briefly looked at her. She smiled too.

The weather was pretty good that day. The air was warm, even though winter was round the corner. So I opened the window to let her enjoy the breeze. In between looking at the road and focusing on driving, I looked at her. She was looking out of the window most of the time. Her face was serene and it appeared that with that breeze, she was letting her bad memories go away. I didn't say anything and let her enjoy. The early morning was tinged with a mysterious blue mistiness. The road in front was wide open, like life stretched before me, alluring me to live every moment.

We drove for about two hours before we reached the lake.

I parked the car in the parking lot, which was almost empty, barring a couple of other cars. One look at the lake a few metres away had the caliber to drive away all the sadness and infuse an unsaid energy. The lake was surrounded by trees all around and there was a circular narrow path lined along the trees. There were wooden benches a little away from this path for visitors to rest on. Most of the benches were unoccupied, because not many people had reached so early. Few elderly people were jogging around the lake. I could also see a couple sitting hidden behind the bushes, and it wasn't very difficult to guess what they were up to. Avoiding all these distractions, I held her hand and led her to the embankment of the lake.

"Okayyyy," she said looking at me with fond love, letting out her breath that she had been holding for a long time. "So this is your surprise."

"Yes, it's just the beginning," I said, facing her. She wasn't looking at me; she was mesmerized with the lake. But I was looking at her, observing every single emotion that flashed on her face in such a short span of time. I could see that she was trying to believe that all this was true. When the feeling and the beauty around had sunk in, she just whispered, "It's a beautiful place, Sanjeev. Thank you for bringing me here."

Just then, as if she had been suffused with some invisible energy, she started running and looked back to say, "Come, come...catch me!" I started running after her. After some running, she was out of breath. She bent down and put her hands on her knees, to rest. I stopped running and went closer to her. She stumbled and fell on me.

"Caught you," I said lovingly, smiling at her.

"Yes, but only because I let myself be caught." We both laughed at that and I hugged her. It was the best feeling in the world to hold someone you love. I could feel her heart beating close to mine, her breath on my neck and her tender hands on my back. When she pulled back and looked at me, I saw all the love in her eyes that I had been craving for.

We walked around the lake, ate at the cafeteria in the premises and lay on the grass looking at the sky for very long. Somewhere in between, we called Ruchita to check if she'd be joining us. She teasingly asked us to have a good time and refused to be the *kabaab mein haddi*. Before we realized, the day's end lay in the tender glow of the evening. The sun was setting on the other side of the horizon, leaving the sky in a deep orange hue. The breeze was cooler again and it would be dark soon.

We lay on the grass, looking at the sky. I asked her, "What are you afraid of?"

I almost felt her breathing stop, it had become so heavy. She said, with a heavy voice, "I am afraid of losing my mom. Afraid of losing this life. Losing everyone I love. I have lost once." I wondered for a second if that 'everyone' included me as well, but I didn't ask. In fact, I didn't say anything. In about five more minutes, I could sense her breath had stabilized.

She asked me, "What about you? What are you afraid of?" I knew this question would come, but didn't know if I was prepared to handle it.

"Me? I think it's the feeling of unrequited love that I am most afraid of. And maybe I am also afraid of dying without being loved by anyone again." My tone seemed oppressed by a dead melancholy.

"Do you believe in soulmates?" Shuchi asked.

I didn't respond for a moment. She nudged me and said, "I asked you something."

"Sorry. I was lost. What did you ask?" I said, coming out of my dead melancholy.

"You believe in soulmates?"

It reminded of Gaurav's words a few months back. *He was right. That time I wasn't so confident of this words, but having Shuchi in my life now, I had to agree that Gaurav was right.*

"Yes, I do." I turned my head and looked into her eyes.

She smiled and said, "You know what, now…me too."

For a moment, we were both silent. Then our reverie was broken by the sudden chirruping of birds. They must be returning home as night was about to fall. I looked at her, but she didn't look at me. Her gaze was locked on the birds, as if she was trying to feel the chirping. She whispered, still seemingly lost in her thoughts. "They are going home. Isn't it beautiful? The sound of birds chirping."

"Yes, it is. It's evening. And they are going back to their nests. To spend time with their loved ones," I replied without looking at her.

The serenity of the whole situation brought out a melancholy in me that I had been trying hard to hide till now. I did not even realize when but I started speaking unknowingly. As if the world didn't mean a thing to me and this serenity was all that mattered.

"Shuchi, I am broken. Something that I find very hard to explain. I am a fucked up person, emotionally. And you know what, I don't know how to fix myself up. It seems this damage is irreparable, as if some part of me has broken forever and nothing would ever bring it back to what it was. Like a broken toy…toys that no one wants to keep with themselves. I have tried to heal myself, but have failed miserably. Sometimes I am haunted with the thought that I will die with this feeling of unrequited love. I don't want to hurt anyone, least of all you. I wish I could promise you perfect days and sunshine, but I don't know if I will ever be able to take the place in your heart that Rohan had…" My words trailed off brokenly.

She looked at me with a sudden jerk; it was so sudden that I noticed it from the corner of my eye and looked at her.

"Sanjeev, in case you haven't noticed, I am broken too," she said but stopped suddenly, as if she wanted to say something more, but her throat choked with the words.

I wanted to kiss her and tell her how much she meant to me and how much I was enjoying this day. But I wasn't so sure how she would react to this. We had kissed earlier, but it was so hard for me to touch her now, to hold her hand. As if the wall of our broken feelings had created this invisible rift in us in this moment. I was brooding over this when I saw

Shuchi coming closer to me. My heart pounded, seeing her face so close to mine. She looked beautiful, her smile full of a subtle charm; love lurking in the depth of her eyes. I saw a smile on the corner of her lips. My heart pounded, now slowly. The stolid silence started evaporating and she kissed me. It was a kiss of reassurance, a kiss of faith in feelings, a kiss that stopped time for a few minutes, a kiss which restored the feeling of being honest for her, a kiss that let my fear of unrequited love pass away, to give way to the heralding of new sunshine for me.

She broke the kiss, but didn't go away. Her forehead touched mine and our noses also touched deliciously. "Shuchi, I love you."

She didn't say anything. But her eyes spoke. It was sheer, exuberant, instinctive, unreasoning, careless joy. And for me, seeing all these feelings on her face brought ecstasy to my heart after so many years of desolation.

We held hands and lay down again, feeling unsaid words and emotions. New dreams began to take over our imagination and we both fell into a dreamy silence. Slowly, stars started coming into the sky. It was magical to see them sparkling one after the other.

"You know, I always wanted to do this. Lying down on the grass and looking at the stars. It makes me happy," she said.

I smiled and began humming some tune that came to my mind. It seemed like an eternity had passed with each other under the open sky. We could hear crickets in the grass although the lake surroundings were well lit. At around 7.30 p.m., when everyone started leaving and the lake began to look deserted, we also decided to leave. I pulled the car out of the parking and she came and sat next to me. We both were silent, not because of awkwardness of some kind, but rather the feeling of love. We left for Delhi and the last surprise for the day was the great Chinese food at a restaurant on the way. I had already made the reservations and we were given a table in the garden. There was a fountain next to the table and live soft instrumental music playing close by. It was breathtakingly beautiful and very apt for a romantic candle light dinner. I served her the food that I had already ordered while making the booking over a phone call. The dessert was our favourite – a chocolate walnut brownie with hot chocolate sauce, and a dollop of vanilla ice cream on top, garnished with cashews and almonds. Our eyes gorged on the dessert before our tongues did.

We left an hour later and headed towards the city. During the entire drive, her eyes had a twinkle of love and happiness.

We reached Delhi around 10:30 p.m. I had taken half an hour more than what I had promised the travel agent. I dropped Shuchi home as it was already late. Before turning towards her home, she turned towards me and said, "Thank you Sanjeev, for everything." Her lips loosened in an exultant smile, assuring me that the surprise I had planned had panned out beautifully.

She started walking towards the main door of her house. But I didn't want this day to end like this; so simply after the lovely day together. I didn't even know how it had made her feel. I thought I'd stop her and ask her how she had felt, but it wasn't easy. I thought that if she said she'd had a good time today, I would ask her to come over to my place the next day.

Thinking thus, I also came out of the car and said, "Shuchi, wait!"

She stopped and turned around. I fumbled, "Umm…I…I wanted to say…thanks for coming with me. I had a wonderful time today."

She smiled and said softly, "Thanks Sanjeev, for all that you did for me. I would never forget this day." She came closer to me, but I wasn't sure if she would kiss me. I hoped she would. A night like this, the breeze blowing and with her dark black eyes, with her hair down and everything that happened today, I didn't want to miss the opportunity if it came up. Being with her, I had not even realized how the entire day had passed. We looked into each other's eyes. The silence in between us felt so romantic to me. I wished I could dance with her. And when she came so closer to me and gave me a peck on my cheeks, I felt little butterflies in my stomach. But I soon pulled myself when I saw her mother out in the balcony. She must have been waiting for Shuchi. Seeing both of us like that, she smiled.

"Come inside, Sanjeev," she said from there.

"No, aunty. Thank you. It is already so late. I just came to drop her."

"Okay. But do come some other day."

"Sure will."

She walked into the main gate, and I knew life had changed now. For the better. Even though she hadn't responded to my proposal. She might need more time for that, I thought and left for my room.

The next morning, I woke up with a smile. The past day had been wonderful and the times to come would be penned in our memories in gold, I was sure.

Just when I had freshened up and was standing in front of the wardrobe looking at what to wear for office, I received a call from the new manager – who was usually evil – that along with few other colleagues, I had to fly to London for some training. I was shocked at the suddenness, but recalled that our passports had been taken from us when we had joined and this training had been promised in a few months' time. I had completely forgotten about it, and now, here it was!

The flight was to be taken the next morning, and I had but a few hours to pack, collect essential documents from the office and get going. I got to test immediately after discussing the whole thing with Vineet, who was also one of the chosen. He was happy that this team had been selected by the top management on the basis of work performance, and that Mahima hadn't been shortlisted.

My second call was made to Shuchi, but it kept ringing. I thought of informing Ruchita, but her phone was also not answered.

It was the opportunity I had been waiting for. This phone call had made me ecstatic.

Who knew that there would be another phone call from an unknown number that would change my day.

"Hello."

"Hi." A female voice said from the other end. In a second, I recognized the voice. My heartbeat became faster and I felt palpitations. I had always wanted this to happen, but that the call would come at this moment, I had never imagined. It was Ashima.

"How are you?" she asked casually. The anger and madness her voice had the last time we had spoken was gone.

I didn't know what to say, because I didn't want to speak to her. All the memories flashed in front of me. But I also knew that I won't be able to avoid her.

"I am good. How come you decided to call after so many years?" I asked.

"Well, I will not mince my words, Sanjeev. I wanted to apologize."

I was surprised.

"For what?"

"I know I have hurt you a lot and you were so broken that you wrote a book about us. And I never contacted you. The way I had spoken to you last time, I know a mere sorry won't be enough, but I want to say that I was wrong every single moment and you were right. I ditched you for someone else and he ditched me for someone else. He was the biggest jerk."

I listened to her with rapt attention. So a lesson had been taught and she had learnt it the hard way, just like me. I didn't know what to say, but was sure about one thing – I wasn't going back to my old life, no matter what.

She continued, "I shouldn't have cheated you like this. Now I realize that you were a gem of a person, and I lost a diamond while collecting stones."

"Ashima, whatever happened in the past has been left behind in the past. There was no doubt that I loved you..." Before I could complete the sentence, she interrupted.

"Loved? You don't love me anymore?" she asked.

It seemed that everything was a joke for her. When she wanted to leave me, she did. And now that she wanted to come back, she thought she could do that too. It made me furious.

"What do you want, Ashima?" I asked in a stern tone.

"I want you. The way things were with us. The same again."

"This world doesn't work the way you want it to. It has been so many years since we fell apart, and for me, there is no turning back. I pleaded to you at that time. You insulted me and left me alone. I struggled for all this while. I spent all these years doing nothing but ruining myself. Can you count how many nights seven years has? It's simple to calculate: two thousand five hundred and fifty-five days and nights. Can you calculate the number of hours? Sixty-one thousand three hundred and twenty hours. Even if someone takes eight hours thinking every night, can you calculate the number of seconds someone has thought about you? Seven crore thirty-five lakhs eighty-four thousand. Can you calculate the number of moments in those seconds? Can you? You can't! Because it can't be calculated. It's not a number that can be easily calculated by pushing a few buttons on your calculator."

"I am sorry, Sanjeev. But I can't find another you."

"Sorry, Ashima. You chose to part ways with me long ago. Our paths are different now. Please don't call me again." For a moment, the silence grew stolid and before she could offer another explanation, I disconnected the phone.

It seemed like the burden that I had been carrying for so long was over now. I felt light. The words that I wanted to tell her on what damage she had done to me, I finally had.

Suddenly I heard a girl's voice. "Hello, Mr Watson! Where are you lost?"

I looked around, surprised to see Ruchita at the door.

"She called me," I said, without any smile.

"Who?" she paused and asked. "Wait…Ashima?"

"Yes."

"What does she want now?"

"She wants to come back."

Her face was devoid of expressions, just like mine. "And what did you say?"

"There is no coming back."

"That's good." She softened her quivering smile listening to this.

"What else is new?"

"I am flying to London for a training cum conference."

"That's awesome. When? And for how long?"

"Tomorrow morning…for a month."

"Did you tell Shuchi? She will be upset about this."

"I called her, but she wasn't available. Have dropped a message."

Ruchita said she would leave for college, as she had dropped by just to say hello. And also to tease me about the day out with Shuchi. But hearing about Ashima's call, she had reserved the teasing for some other day. I came out with Ruchita till the building gate to say goodbye, because I knew I would meet her only after a month now.

Just then, I saw a bouquet lying in a dustbin nearby.

"See this! It seems someone broke someone's heart. And the bouquet in the dustbin was the witness."

I packed up my stuff and collected all the necessary documents, in between calling Shuchi a number of times. I called her on the mobile, on the land phone, but she wasn't available. Finally I called up her mother and asked her where Shuchi was. She said she didn't know as she was at the bank and would be home only in the evening. She told me Shuchi must have back to back classes in college, so I decided to call later.

I called her up the entire time I was in the cab going to the airport, then from the airport waiting lounge, and even when we had boarded. I just couldn't get through to her and helplessly had to switch my phone off.

It had been weeks and I had not been able to speak to Shuchi. I had left numerous messages, called a hundred times. Now, even her mother was not picking up the phone.

We were sitting in the conference when Vineet suddenly bent a little closer to me and said, "Are you fine buddy?"

"Yeah! Why are you asking?" I looked at him, holding my coffee.

He straightened up and said a moment later, looking at my phone, sipping his coffee, "Just that you've been staring at your phone since the morning. Even during the meeting with the manager, your focus was somewhere else. Are you expecting some important call or message?"

I looked at my phone. I was still fiddling with it. I realized it was true that I was waiting for Shuchi's call or message, but I couldn't share it with anyone. I looked at him, put a fake smile on my face and said with a suppressed smile, 'Aah, no no! I have somehow acquired this nasty habit of playing with my phone all the time. Everything is fine."

He smiled but it didn't look so assuring. What else could I have said anyway? To distract him from this issue, I asked, "The training going on is pretty well, no?"

He suddenly looked charged up. "Oh yes, definitely. I also think so, but the real pain is making presentations at the end. Not just that, we have to present them in front of an entire team to grab better projects."

"True that! But now, since the training has been done so well, it seems like an easy task."

Just then, another colleague named Sameer came and joined us. We were talking about the projects that were due to be released soon and were looking and getting to work on those in most demand. I made a remark about how Mahima would stand the best chance of getting the desired project and Vineet got pissed again. I stood up to throw the cup in the dustbin when Sameer asked in a very excited tone, "Hey, Sanjeev. I heard you are an author. Heard people talking about you. Is it true?"

That made me stop in my tracks and I turned around to look at him. I never liked the last part of this question. How hard is it for someone to just Google my name and picture if they have heard something about me? Also because this one question is just the beginning of an entire range of questions that follow. But I knew well I couldn't make other people understand this. So, to avoid any such awkward situation, I just smiled and said,

"Yes, it's true."

"Wow! That's so cool man. How do you get time to write? And how many books have you written so far?"

As expected, so many questions in one go. I always hated this. Now, neither did I want to seem like a snooty author, nor was I in a mood to humour him. So I just said, "We will discuss this later during lunch time." I continued half laughing, "Let's go and attend this business ethics seminar first."

The lecture was almost an hour long and it was boring as hell. There was no notification on my phone that could indicate Shuchi's call or message; that made the one hour look like one year. I checked my phone two or three times in between, but there was nothing.

This had been going on for weeks now. I would wait for her calls or messages, and would get none. A day began with hopes and ended with disappointment. Whenever I tried calling her, her phone was either out of reach or switched off. I had even tried calling on her land phone, but the same had been the case. It kept ringing and ringing and ringing, but nobody answered. Because of all this, I grew so impatient that I just wanted to get home. But I still had a week in between. I had already gotten the tickets to Delhi booked on the earliest possible flight after the training.

I had not involved Ruchita in between this, lest she thought there was some major problem, but I guess that had been a bad decision.

At the end of that day, I called her up as soon as the seminar ended. She answered excitedly in her usual energetic tone, "Hey, Mr Author. How are you and when are you coming back to Delhi?"

"Hi Ruchita. I am good. How about you? I am coming back this Sunday night."

"Wow. Cool. Come soon. We will party again like old times."

"Sure." My mind was occupied with some other thought and was waiting patiently to come to it.

I asked hesitantly, "Do you have any idea about Shuchi? I've tried calling her so many times, but haven't been able to connect."

"Did you talk to her even once after you left? She was devastated."

"Why?"

"Actually she came to your room that day when I was there too and overheard your conversation with Ashima. She thought you are going back to her again. Since she knew from your book that you really loved Ashima, she didn't want to come in between the two of you. In fact, that bouquet we saw in the dustbin…she had gotten it for you. She had come to say yes to your proposal, Sanjeev. After that, she just locked herself in her room and didn't talk to anyone."

"Oh god! This has been a huge misunderstanding. Then?"

"When she didn't talk to me for a long time, I went to her home and clarified the situation. She was relieved after listening to me. I also told her you are in London and she was feeling silly that she had wasted so much time. I thought she'd have called you after that. I am surprised she didn't."

"Thanks Ruchita. I can't lose her this way… not to a misunderstanding. She is the centre of my universe. For me the entire universe merges into one point and that point is Shuchi. You know that."

"Yes, I know very well."

"But still I didn't hear from her. It has been almost three weeks. No calls. No messages. I am so worried. I am not feeling good at all. My heart sinks thinking about her absence. I just want to leave this bullshit seminar and fly back to India to see her."

"You know what, even I tried calling her a few days back, but her phone number is unavailable," she said.

"Tried calling her? Means? You haven't met her in college?" I asked surprised.

"No, I am not in Delhi either. I am in Punjab with my family to attend a wedding. It's my closest cousin, so I have been here for the last two weeks."

"Oh! When will you be back?"

"A day before you…by Saturday."

"Okay, great! Let's catch up and find out what this devil is trying to hide from us," I said light-heartedly, though only on the surface. Inside me, there was a storm brewing, worrying me sick about Shuchi. The impatience that had grown within me in these three weeks was killing me. I had no other way to reach her.

After bidding adieu to other fellows attending the seminar, I hopped onto the flight back to Delhi. Even though the flight was almost ten hours long, it was no match to my impatience and seemed much longer. I wanted to reach as soon as possible and wanted to see Shuchi. Once I landed at the Delhi Airport, I messaged Ruchita to confirm if she had reached Delhi or not. The message didn't get delivered.

It was past midnight. It was a cold winter night and visiting Shuchi now would not be a great idea. I didn't even have Ruchita to help me scale the wall and hop into her apartment this time. It would have scared anyone. So I decided to head home and visit Shuchi the first thing the next morning. As I alighted from the cab and reached the letterbox, the guard who manned the entry gate greeted me. He saluted and said, "There were a few parcels for you when you were gone, sir. Please sign here." I signed without looking because I was wondering who would have sent me parcels. And what could they contain. Parcels always excited me. He handed me a few packets and one box. I rushed to my room and started reading the letters one by one. There were bills, bank statements, and various other documents. Among other letters, there was a special envelope waiting for me. I kept everything else aside and picked up the thick envelope. It was from Shuchi. And it had arrived a day back.

My tiredness evaporated the moment I opened the envelope. There were at least ten pages inside the packet, all of them inked. Each page had a number written on it. I presumed that Shuchi wanted me to read those pages according to the number on them, in chronological order.

I was hopeful that this letter was full of love for me; she must have missed me. But it made me suspicious too. Why hadn't she picked up my phone or called if she was missing me?

Anyway, I geared up for the long reading session and I wanted to savour every single word she had written for me, like a connoisseur savours art. I switched on the heater, took off my blazer, removed my shoes and sat on the sofa.

The room was quiet and I could easily hear my heart beating.

My mind was abuzz with questions. Why did she write so many pages? She could have called me or messaged me. Why did she disappear without letting anyone know about her? Where is she? Did she wait for me to go to send this letter? But how did she come to know that I was travelling?

There was only one way to find out, and I dived into the letter to uncover the truth.

1.

Dear Sanjeev,

When one misses someone deeply, do you know what they do? They recall all the conversations they have ever shared, all the times they have spent together, all the fun they have had and all the moments that they have turned into precious memories. I am going to do just that through these letters.

Don't cheat, ok! Read them one by one. There are numbers on each page.

You may be wondering why I am writing these letters to you. Not one, not two, but I am sure they'd be more. But I feel it's important and this is the right time. Yes, I could have said these things to you in person, but since the day I have read your book and met you, I wanted to know how it feels to express things in writing and how different it is from expressing something face to face. I told you I had written an article earlier, remember? And that it had gotten really awful reviews? I hope this one gets good reviews ;) So it's the first time for me, and kind of different too.

So tell me? Do you want to know about things from the first day we met or even before that? Maybe everything in random order?

Oh, come on! Who wants randomness in life? Well…Me! It brings excitement in life. So here it goes!

After I broke up with Rohan, my brain stopped working for sometime. The reality was too painful for me to live with. It was not just about my broken heart, but my broken faith too. And also the wounded ability to trust anyone and love again. Being with him had opened the doors to a whole new world for me. Out of love, I said yes for everything. We went out, bunked classes, went to parties and met people I didn't sometimes like. For several months, it was full of new feelings and excitement. He held my hand and made me experience many new things. But after he tried to force himself upon me, I didn't want to see his face. I would have imagined that he was drunk and had tried to get physical with me in a state of drunkenness, but his unapologetic stand even after he was sober angered me. I realized he was a playboy, and had never really loved me. I was an object for him, but one that did not wish to accept just anything he wished to do.

College life became easier because he was in the final year and all the mess happened just a few weeks before he was to pass out. Still, I barely attended college those days in a fear that I'd see him again. I just went to college for the final exams. And then also, my mother took leave from office to accompany me. I had told her everything and she stood by me like a rock. I am sure you know this, but I love her a lot. The day I broke up with him and was crying all day and night in my room, it was mom who cheered me up again and said something that I still remember. She said, "If a guy holds your hand and your heart beats faster, and there are butterflies in your stomach, run away from him. He won't be the best partner for you. But if a guy holds your hand and you feel warm, secure and strong, he is the right person for you." When she had said this, I had looked at her strangely. She told me that she had made the same mistake. Rohan had made my heart beat faster, and she understood that it was infatuation. She narrated how she had felt the same way about a guy in her college. She had, in fact, married him and it hadn't worked out.

2.

It made me sadder that her life revolved around me only. My father had been sweet to me, never talked rudely and always brought presents or chocolates for me. I wanted to ask mom how things went ugly, but I could never gather the courage to do that. Every time he visited us, it was followed by a heated argument in a closed room for some thirty odd minutes before he came out furious. On his way back, he would smile at me and leave while mom would be crying in the room. For several years, I couldn't understand how it could happen. How can someone claim to be in love and still leave her? I inferred two things out of it – either he never loved her and was with her in the same way like Rohan, or love fades with time and everything becomes boring. Either way, it's miserable for the people at the other end. Finally, before my 10th board exams, they both decided to part ways, and I never saw him again.

Losing someone is very hard, isn't it? Because when you lose someone who was once so close, it's like losing yourself. I know you know this better than me. You have suffered the pain that I could sense in your book.

I know that there were several questions in your mind the day I shouted at Rohan. You have never seen me like this. How could a nice and quiet girl like me shout at someone like that! But I don't act like this usually. I was a sweet girl when I joined Delhi University.

Anyhow, when we moved into the second year of college, for several months, I wasn't interacting with any students. A few girls who knew about me and Rohan came to sympathize with me, but for some reason, I couldn't gel with them. I couldn't make any friends. Girls from my class used to hang out with other classmates, but I never went out. Weekends were always for my mom. She cooks delicious food, so I gorged on it on weekends. Sometimes, I cooked her favourite dinner and we laughed, chit-chatted, gossiped and even teased each other. She accompanied me when I went shopping as well. I remember I didn't ask her once, and went shopping with Rohan without telling her. He wanted to gift me some lingerie. So it was kind of secret. He gifted me some very expensive lingerie that day. I hesitated initially, but he was adamant. I didn't want to hurt his feelings, so I accepted it. And this was the only thing I didn't tell mom. I felt a little embarrassed. But after the break-up, I burnt every single thing he had given to me. Teddy bears, cards, clothes, lingerie and several pieces of artificial jewelry. After that evening, all those gifts looked like a bribe to sleep with him. To impress me and to make me so crazy about him that he could do anything he wanted with me, without my having any objection. It was disgusting. How can someone play with feelings like this?

3.

I also realized a few good things because of this episode – Life always goes on and no one cares about you anymore, except those few people who have always loved you. And that there will always be some people who will love you. I realized that infatuation is a powerful feeling that can make the wisest of people go blind to other aspects of life. I had done that too. When I was with Rohan, for several weeks, I didn't spend my weekends with mom. She didn't say anything. In fact, she was happy to see me spending time with someone else. I wanted him to meet my mom, but for some reason, he never came home. Maybe he just wanted to sleep with me and wanted to break up with me after that. I still feel sorry that for a bastard like him, I didn't give the due attention and time to my mom. It was cruel on my part. And not just mom, another person who really cared for me was Swati, who I had befriended in the very first year of college. We had a good tuning and always used to play pranks on others. Before Rohan came into my life, I spent most of my time with her. Even when a bigger group from our class went out for a movie, I always chose to sit beside her so that I could laugh and share popcorn with her. I felt free with her. I feel any relationship is all about freedom, isn't it? But after Rohan came into my life, I couldn't give much time to her. All of a sudden, he became my priority. She called me several times, pinged me on WhatsApp. I talked to her, but only for a few seconds. When she asked me to go out for movies or shopping with her, I made excuses. She caught me red-handed once when I had refused to go with her on the pretext of being unwell, when I had really gone out with Rohan. Despite that, she didn't say anything at that time, but she never talked to me again. Initially I didn't realize her absence, but after the break-up, I found that there was no one to talk to. I shouldn't have done this with her. I had made someone a priority who totally didn't deserve it, and ignored everyone who truly cared for me. It happens. You must have experienced it too, I am sure. I read it in the book…how you three were good friends but by the end of the second year, everything had fallen apart.

4.

It was a long time after the break-up that I picked up your novel. My mom always encouraged me to read books. It was during the mall visit one evening that I walked into a bookstore. After flipping through several pages in the store, it was the red petals on the cover that caught my attention. I had a hard time pulling out the book from the shelf. It was behind a few books, and for me it proved to be a hidden treasure. Your name was unknown to me, but it didn't matter. The title, In Course of True Love, *intrigued me. It was kind of cute. So I bought a copy.*

That night, I finished dinner early and came directly to my room. I picked up the book and read the entire book overnight. Seeing the lights on, my mom came several times to check if I was crying, but seeing me reading a book made her smile. She came and pulled a chair to sit next to me. She asked me about the book and the author. I told her this was your first book and I had bought it that evening. She took the book and glanced over it, and gave it back to me.

"Today when I went to your college to pay the fees, I saw a poster about a writing competition. Are you planning to participate in it?" she asked me.

"I guess not." I had never written and had no plans of doing so.

"Why? I loved the article you had written in the college magazine. And I recall you were so excited to write it and then seeing it getting published in the DU newspaper."

"Yes, but it was tough to write. It took four days to write and at last what I got was only harsh criticism in return."

"Oh, but I loved it. People might not have understood the subtle sarcasm you had put in."

"Mom, I know you are saying this because you don't want to hurt me."

"And if you are so afraid of people, why don't you start a blog? It would be a good idea." She was in no mood to give up that day.

"And what would I be writing there?"

"Anything you love to share. And sometimes, I could also post as a guest on something like 'how to have a lovely daughter even when you are a single mother'," she teased.

"Very funny, mom. But I don't know. Will tell you once I make up my mind. Now let me read this novel." She kissed me on my forehead like every night and closed the door behind her.

Once I started reading your book, I stopped only after finishing it. By the time I finished reading, it was 3 a.m. I found myself sobbing. I felt bad for you. It was a heart-breaking story and somewhere while reading, I felt connected to it. Just like you, I had been cheated too. Just like love was so important for you, it was for me as well. Just like you, my friendship with others had also fallen apart. And like you, there was some disappointment from the parents' side – just one parent in my case though. Your story appeared in front of me and it seemed that it was me living this story. With your loss, I left I had lost something too. Those innocent voices that I could hear in my mind, that passionate love for her and your wailing in a childlike manner touched my heart. I wanted to know you more, to know your story and what happened next. Immediately, I switched on the laptop, typed a message and sent it to you.

5.

For the next two days, I waited for you reply, but there came none. I felt sad. In those two days, I checked your Facebook profile a million times, but there were no updates as well. To know more about you, I checked your photographs and posts. There were a few pictures of your novel, and an old pic in which you looked like a child. I read every single post till your first status. It was mostly emotional and romantic posts. I thought of dropping a message there, but seeing no recent activities, I didn't.

In the college as well, I wanted to tell everyone how much I had loved this new novel and carried it with me that day. A few got excited, but most didn't show any interest as they were not into reading fiction. In the recess, I kept re-reading the novel when someone said to me, "I can see you keep reading the same novel. You're in love with this book!" And I replied, "With the author as well and his story." But I was sad as you hadn't replied. Yet I didn't want to look desperate.

Even on the breakfast table, I kept refreshing my mail in vain. My mom noticed this and asked me, "What's this, Shuchi? You keep checking your phone every now and then. What's up?"

"Nothing mom. I had sent a mail to Sanjeev after reading his novel. It has been two days but he hasn't replied yet. I am getting restless now."

She asked me after some thought, "Did you send him a message on Facebook?"

"No, mom. For the past several weeks, there has been no activity on his Facebook wall. Don't know where he is. Or just ignoring my mail."

"Don't feel dejected. Give him at least three days to reply before you form an opinion. He must be busy. By the way, I forgot to ask how the novel was."

"Mom, he is also broken like me, but his feeling of unrequited love seems to be killing him daily. His mom doesn't love him as well. So that must be so difficult."

She remained silent. I made a mental note to give him a day more to reply, but if he didn't reply even then, I would be so restless. Despite all this, I kept checking my mails and Facebook again and again. When till the evening there was no reply from your side, I made a fake account to mail you again in case you had forgotten to reply to my email or were ignoring me. I didn't know what the scene was like so I was just trying all my options. Seeing a new mail may remind you of my earlier mail, I thought. I drafted the mail in a different way so that you couldn't guess that it was me.

Just as my mom had said, my phone vibrated a few minutes before midnight. I checked it at once. It was your mail! I was on cloud nine and felt like going to mom's room and kissing her. I excitedly opened the mail and read every word, but it was only a formal thank you note. You hadn't answered anything that I had asked in the mail. It was only mentioned that you felt great that I loved the book and it made you smile. It looked like you had copied your standard reply to your fans and readers and had edited the name and pasted it. It disappointed me, but I felt happy to see your reply. I jumped towards the laptop and within an instant mailed you again, thinking you'd still be online and this time, I would be getting the reply instantly. There would be chances to know more if we could exchange emails instantly. I drafted the mail. This was the fastest I had ever typed. I was excited about your reply and kept staring at the laptop screen, refreshing Gmail several times. But again, no reply. It irritated me so much. This time I didn't get any reply in the next six days. I made several fake accounts and often mailed you differently to ask you several questions, but though you did reply to most of the emails, I was never fully satisfied. I had even asked you in the mail that if you'd come to Delhi, could you please inform on Facebook, so that I could meet you. But you never came for a book launch. After about a month or so, I stopped checking those accounts.

6.

You know, the day Ruchita told me she was your friend, I felt so jealous. How could it be possible that you were in Delhi and hadn't informed anyone! For a moment, I got so furious, but I knew I couldn't ask Ruchita as she didn't know anything about it. I had never spoken to her before that. I requested Ruchita to ask you to meet me just once, and she agreed. That evening, a smile spread on my face after so long. When my mom saw me so happy, she asked me, "My daughter looks so happy. What's the occasion?"

"Mom, can you believe Sanjeev is in Delhi?"

"That's awesome. Did he mail you?"

"No, Ruchita told me. She is a friend from college, and met him in a photography class. They are very good friends. Luckily, she had once seen me bragging about Sanjeev in the canteen and she remembered it. So she asked me about it," I said excitedly.

"And?" she asked happily.

"And I requested her to ask Sanjeev to meet me and she has agreed. Isn't she sweet?"

"Yes, she is. Sanjeev will not say no to her, I am sure, and will definitely meet you." Whenever my mom says things like these, I feel assured. Most of the time, she is correct about her predictions. That night, I read your book again. Every single detail. I wanted to talk to you about every unanswered question in the book. I even started preparing a series of questions to ask you. The night you replied agreeing to meet me, I was ecstatic and over the moon. I ran towards my mom's room and woke her up in the middle of the night to tell her. It was quite a mad rush kind of thing for me. I couldn't sleep that night. Mom came in at around 4 a.m. and asked me to sleep. I had been thinking what I was going to wear, how you would look in person, what we could talk about and such things. I wanted to look my best. I rummaged through my entire wardrobe, but I found something amiss in every outfit.

There was still a day to go before we met, so I decided that I would go and get a new dress. That too red. It is your favourite colour, isn't it?

I made a note of all the questions I'd ask you and then went shopping.

Are you going to write another book?

How could she leave when you loved her so much?

Are you seeing anyone currently?

I am not that stupid to ask you embarrassing questions, so thought I'd ask questions in a subtle way. I didn't want to scare you, after all. That evening, I picked up the best dress I could buy. Seeing me, mom got excited as well.

7.

Mom wanted to drop me to Connaught Place, but I insisted on going on my own.

I got late because of an accident near Karol Bagh. Stupid people! They can't even drive properly. I didn't realize that you were waiting for me. I thought you might come late. Because once I had been to a book launch just to see how it feels to witness being with an author. The author had come in an hour late. By that time, most of the readers had left the event. But you were there, waiting for me. I was embarrassed to have kept you waiting.

That evening when we met, it was so nice of you to pull the chair out for me. When I sat and had a look at you, I still couldn't believe that I was sitting right in front of you. Right in front of you. I wondered if I would ever tell you how I had rehearsed this entire scene in the last two days. I had imagined it in my head so many times. I always thought what I would say, what I would do, how it would all turn out to be. I didn't want to sound or look stupid in front of you, but I was so nervous around you. And guess what? You were equally nervous, though you tried your best to hide it. I couldn't understand it in the first guess; I presumed you'd have met readers on regular basis. After all, you must have been getting so many fan mails and messages on social media. You could also be arrogant for all I know, because you hadn't answered my mails, not all of them at least. But it turned out to be exactly the opposite.

I found that you are a quiet person, like someone who comes into a class and sits alone in the corner. And then tops at the end. There was no air of arrogance around you, perhaps some nervousness. You were so humble and it felt like you were still suffering from the burden of your memories. Our entire conversation went in a completely different way than I had imagined it to be.

8.

When I came back, I felt really good. I recalled how I used to be irritated when you weren't replying to my emails, or replying briefly, but it seemed to me that destiny had planned it differently. Something bigger than just getting a reply to an email.

It occurred to me that if I ever met you, it would be at some formal book launch event. But like this? It was beyond my imagination. Patience has its own reward, I guess.

It took me by surprise how politely you talked to me. Even those questions that made you uncomfortable, you refused to answer cutely. Above all, that cake with chocolate sauce was super tasty. I was glad to see such warm hospitality from you. I felt like the luckiest being. In the first impression, you seemed so quiet and gentle.

And now, it often fills me with surprise at how precisely you planned the entire day out for me by that lake. It was the biggest gift one can ever give, Sanjeev. I never expressed all this to you, but I also feel deeply for you. The kind of feelings my mom always talked to me about. The feeling of warmth and security. You know Sanjeev, there are many instances when you don't say many things and I understand without your saying it. Your eyes reveal everything. One has to just know how to read your eyes to understand you. It says many things when you feel so much. Plus, eyes cannot lie.

9.

I wanted to say yes to your proposal at that very moment by the lakeside, but I delayed it. I wanted to think over it some more. Next day, I reached your room to say that I love you too, but I overheard your conversation with Ashima. I had read so much about your love for her that I thought you'd want her to be back in your life. It broke my heart totally. I felt you had cheated on me, lied to me. And all these months you had spent with me were nothing but a façade of love. I returned that day without telling you that I was there. Your door was open and you were talking on the phone looking outside the window. I had even brought flowers, which ultimately landed in the dustbin. For the next two days, I locked myself in my room. Even my mom got worried because I didn't talk to anyone, and didn't even go to college. You called me so many times. I was scared that you were calling up to tell me that you're going back to Ashima. My mom was unable to understand what was going on. When she insisted a lot, I told her. I don't know what made her say that, but she said that it couldn't be true. That I must hear you out. I should know the reality before I take a decision. But the fear of those words about Ashima was holding me back. I had found love with such pain and after so long. I didn't want to lose you.

Ruchita had also been calling me continuously and when I didn't receive her calls, she came to my house. That's when she realized what the matter was and why I wasn't responding to anyone. She told me that I had listened to half of your conversation. That although Ashima had called and wanted to come back to you, you had refused flatly and even asked her to never call you back. I felt so relieved, but at that same time I felt so sorry for torturing you. I am sorry, Sanjeev.

Being with you, I learnt again how to feel loved. Earlier, it had died within me, the spirit to live and love. Your coming into my life stirred my soul like no one had done before. Like a quick shiver had ruffled the brooding stillness of water. When things went wrong with my parents, my emotions died; but Rohan stirred it again. I mistook the infatuation as love and allowed him to crush it once more. But after you came into my life, it turned out to be so different. That evening when we were walking in the park, I didn't know how, but I blurted out something that was held up inside me for so long. You didn't just listen to it silently, but also made a mental note of it and took care of it. You wanted to enjoy with me in a breeze; you know I liked birds chirping and that's why you took me to the lake so early in the morning. You never intruded in my life because I don't like chaos, and ensured that things took their normal course to settle down.

After spending time with you, I realized that you are a mature person, and I started loving it. There would be several reasons why I'd want to spend time with you. But eventually, it's unconditional and true that I have fallen for you. Every feeling comes out from somewhere deep inside my heart when it's for you. I feel addicted to you and can't think of survival without you now. You touched the strings of my heart that had been abused by many in the past. I want to have you in front of my eyes every single moment and hug you to keep you close to my heart. I want to keep looking into your eyes because they say they love me a million times. I find my small world complete around you. You bring me out of me. You are peace. You are fun. You are support. You are knowledge. You are love. You are life. I wish I never disappoint and hurt you, because it will hurt me too. Since you are not in the city, I find letters to be the best way to express things. I want you to know how special you are for me and how lucky I feel to have you. And how much I love you – truly and deeply. You are the loveliest gift of god to me and I owe you this best phase of my life.

Love,
Shuchi

I could not help but smile. She had been honest with me from the very beginning of our relationship, but this letter was her heart wrenched open. She had bared herself to me the way I could have never imagined. She loved me, yes! And in a way that completed me. I had always missed true love in my life, and she was now the link that filled the void. My life was finally complete and I wanted to hug her just then. Right there. Right then. I wanted to hold her close and tell her I would never let her go. That she would be a part of me that gives me a reason to live. I missed her and wanted to tell her how much I loved her. I flipped over to the last couple of pages. The letter wasn't in continuation, but a fresh one.

10.

Dear Sanjeev,

Over the times that we have spent together, I have grown fond of you. You are not like any other guy who always tends to flirt.

Spending time with you, I feel liberated and loved. It makes my heart beat faster, but it also makes me feel secure and loved. You may not speak sugar-coated words, but your words touch my heart. I know I have never told you all this in person, but it's better to tell you how I feel rather than keeping it in my heart. Whenever you talked to me, I saw a gentleness and concern in your face, care in your eyes. You are so compassionate. You feel my emotions as gently as if they're your own. Several times, I have caught you looking at me intently, waited for you to say something, sure that you are also afraid to express love like me.

Are you wondering why I have written this and never said it to you? Or why I didn't take your calls or respond to your messages? I am sorry for that, Sanjeev. Because apart from this submission of love, I have something else to say to you. And that is something I couldn't have said in person.

My heart sank. It had all been going so well with her words till now, and this sudden change scared me. What was it that she was going to say? What was it that she couldn't say in person? I quickly got back to the piece of paper and noticed that the handwriting had become different. As if she had written it in a state of extreme tiredness. On reflex, I turned to the first page of the letter. The handwriting was crisp and cursive – beautiful letters crafted with perfection. Turning back to the present page, I saw some letters were scribbled, as if in haste. Was she going somewhere and was in a hurry? I began reading again.

After that morning of the misunderstanding, I was upset and didn't feel like talking to anyone. Unfortunately, your office decided to send you for that seminar just then. Time has been playing tricks with us,

I guess. I was upset, but mom was more upset than I had ever seen her. I asked her what the matter was, and she told me she couldn't see me sad. I hated myself for putting mom through this again, but promised her that I would be fine in a while. I told her I was tired and retired to my room.

That night, something happened in that house that had not happened in the last four years. My dad visited us again. I heard a car screech to a halt in front of the house and I thought some neighbours were parking. But when I heard the door of our house open and close, I got curious. I was watching a romantic movie on my laptop, so I paused it and threw the headphones on the bed before moving out. Just when I came out of my room, I heard the door of mom's room close. It was done softly, as if someone had taken great care to not make any noise. Was mom hiding something from me, I thought. I overheard the voices from the room. It was my father, and he sounded upset. Even mom sounded lost and upset. They were talking very softly, which was completely at odds with how they had talked in the past few years. I came closer and put my ear to the door to hear what was going on.

"Can't there be any other possible way to stop this?" Mom sounded hysterical.

"What can I say? I have tried as much as you have and there seems to be no way out," he said firmly.

"But why don't you understand?" She almost pleaded and I wondered what would have made her so weak in front of the man she disliked so much.

"There is nothing to understand…things have gone too far to make it right again."

I wondered if mom wanted dad to come back into her life. That's what it sounded like. I was confused.

"For our daughter's sake. She is a sign of our love. She doesn't deserve this." She was sobbing. "I beg you...please..." her voice trailed off. I wanted to bang open the door and tell her to stop begging this man. But then I heard his voice, as soft as I never had.

"I understand...I promise I will be with her and fulfil whatever she says."

"Oh god! How will I tell her this?" Her voice froze.

"We will have to do this together," he said.

I was scared that mom would want to be with him again. Did she need a man in her life so bad that she was ready to forsake love and all that she had told me in all these years? This shouldn't be happening.

"What will we tell her? That she has cancer? That she is going to need therapy immediately? That we cannot do anything to help her? How will we answer her questions..." She broke into sobs. And I broke into a cold sweat.

Was this a joke, I thought. If it was, then it was a really bad one! If this turned out to be a prank, I will scold Shuchi so much she'd remember it, I told myself. But then my curiosity beat my sentiments and I continued reading with teary eyes, my hands shivering.

Sanjeev, you know when I heard this, I felt the ground beneath my feet shift. I froze. I had only felt some unease in the past few days. I had been coughing and sneezing, but that's a common cold. It had lingered for long, and made breathing difficult, but that's pollution, right? I was feeling tired too, but isn't that just fatigue! How could I have cancer when I had no symptoms? No pains? Nothing! Tears rolled down my cheeks but I wiped them quickly and ran back to the room. I didn't know what to believe and what not to believe.

After a few more minutes I heard the door close again and a car speeding off. I presumed dad had left. In another twenty minutes, mom knocked at my room door and called me for dinner. I went out after washing my face and tidying my hair, looking as normal as possible.

Mom's eyes looked red and her demeanour was sad. I decided to confront her at the dinner table.

"Mom, can I ask you something? And promise me you won't lie to me."

She was laying out a plate for me and stopped when I said this. She looked at me with horror, as if she was scared if I had known someone was here.

"Yes, beta. Why would I lie to you?" she managed to say with her eyes downcast.

"Mom, am I going to die soon?" Her eyes opened wide when she heard this and tears filled them.

"Who said this to you?" She couldn't hold back the tremor in her voice.

"Mom, don't lie to me. I know I have cancer."

She rushed towards my side and stared into my eyes. She asked in her bewildered tone, "Who said this to you?"

"Mom, I heard you talking to dad." Now I was also teary eyed and knew this would not get any better.

"No, beta. I will save you. You mean the world to me. I will never let anything happen to you. I will get you treated by the best cancer specialists." And she hugged me like never before, breaking into sobs first and then began howling with pain only I could sense. She held me tight – feelings of fear and love overpowering her in the same moment.

"Yes, mom. I trust you. You are the world's best mom." I didn't know at that time whether I would live or die, or how much time I have…but our world shattered into pieces.

The next day we decided to head to the Rajiv Gandhi Cancer Institute so that we could get sound advice and help. I was still coughing and had some problem breathing due to the clogged nose. The crying throughout the night hadn't helped much either.

They admitted me for running some tests and I saw dad there too. After a series of tests that lasted a whole day and the doctors' silence over it, I didn't have very positive thoughts. But I held fort nonetheless to give strength to my mother.

The next morning, mom was nowhere to be seen. Nor was dad, but that was expected. When she came in an hour later, her face said it all. I tried to coax her to reveal what was going on, but she kept crying. I was numb; I could neither cry, nor think. I just wanted to know what was happening. After much coaxing and crying, she told me the reports had confirmed cancer of a rare type. ALL – Acute Lymphoblastic Leukemia. The doctors came in and told me more about it. It happens in youngsters easily and is called acute as it spreads quickly, sometimes in about two weeks. The cough that I had been complaining of was perhaps because of that. And the breathlessness because my lungs had been affected. Scans showed that the cancerous cells had spread to my lungs, uterus and kidneys already and there wasn't much they could do.

Chemotherapy was advised for relief, but I didn't know what was happening. How could my world turn upside down so suddenly? I wanted to meet you, but how would I tell you this? How would you react? After all the pain that you had left behind, how could I throw you into it again?

I know you are returning in a couple of days. And I will be where I have been for a month – the young adult ward of

*Rajiv Gandhi Cancer Institute. I promise I won't cheat on you;
I promise I won't let destiny win over our love; I promise I will
wait for you.*

*Love forever,
Shuchi.*

The moment I finished reading the letter, I heard the
windowpanes hitting the wall hard. I looked out to see
a sudden storm brewing. The weather turned cold, like a
premonition. It began raining and everything hit me like a
sharp pain in the chest.

I had been standing there numb, when my phone rang. It
was Ruchita.

"Sanjeev, I don't know how to say this…" she said in a
broken tone and I could fathom what this could be about.

Before she said anything else, I interrupted her, "I know."

"You know? Did she tell you? I just got call from her
mother. I am so sorry Sanjeev," and she started sobbing.

"She left me some letters where she said everything. I just
finished reading them. I don't know what to do, Ruchita…she
is dying." And the tears that I had been holding back for so long
streamed down.

"Sanjeev, we should go and meet her. I am coming to your
house; just stay where you are. She can't leave you. She can't
leave us like this, goddammit. I am coming." She hurriedly
disconnected the phone.

In the next ten minutes, Ruchita was honking at the main
gate. I was out there waiting for her. We didn't say anything on
our way and she drove as fast as she could.

We checked the room number and rushed towards the room. As we entered the room, Shuchi's mother was there, sitting beside her. Shuchi was lying on the bed. When we entered, she raised her eyes to look at me. A tube was inserted through her mouth, to feed her perhaps. She looked so weak and her face was pale. She had lost quite a lot of weight and in the first glance, I was unable to recognize her. If it wasn't for those deep black eyes, I wouldn't have guessed this to be Shuchi. She had lost her hair as well as her eyebrows because of chemotherapy.

I walked towards her slowly, and could see a tear escape the corner of her eye. Seeing her like this, tears kept pouring out on my cheeks continuously. Unable to hide my pain, I held her hand and started crying.

"Sanjeev, don't cry. I know I don't look beautiful anymore..." she said in a weak voice. Her grip was weak and when I raised my eyes to see her, she was smiling tenderly, although her eyes were full of tears.

"Don't say that, Shuchi. You are the most beautiful girl I have ever known," I said sobbing.

"You know Sanjeev, you can't lie. Everything's visible in your eyes," she said.

She had lost a lot of weight and her skin was frail and dark now. "What's happened to you? Why didn't you tell me about this?"

She smiled through her tears when she heard this.

"Shuchi, you can't leave me like this."

She was finding it quite difficult to speak and with passing time, her voice became too frail to understand. Seeing this, my heart started tightening and my grip over her hands tightened in the fear of losing her. I wanted to stop her from going away from me at any cost.

In her weak voice, she asked me, "Do you love me?"

"Yes, I love you," I said with tearful eyes.

"I love you too, Sanjeev." She forced herself to smile. Seeing her innocent smile and her eyes saying a million things, I brought my face close to hers and kissed her on her forehead.

I looked at her. She had closed her eyes out of fatigue. The situation was so ominous that it scarred my soul. "Sanjeev, you are forever in my heart. I love you," she said meekly. Before taking her final breath, she had uttered those magical words. But it was too late. She closed her eyes forever, her hand in mine.

We all sat beside her – Ruchita continuously crying while I was thinking how much I loved her and the years I would be living without her again. But the most devastated was her mother; she had lost her only companion and the hope to live. It was around six in the morning when Shuchi breathed her last. I was still holding her hand, her other hand in her mother's now. I couldn't feel for a second that she had left me and this world. She looked like a baby who was sleeping. Ruchita came by my side and hugged me tightly, but something had shattered inside me forever. My heart. And my hope.

Two months later

Iwoke up long before dawn and lay exhausted and wakeful, with eyes closed, thinking the countless years I still had to live without her. There are no more missed calls, no more long talks, no more 'I love yous' and giggles. No fights about who will hang up first. No more jokes to giggle about endlessly. No more her. I had reached the same point where I had started a year ago.

Alone. Devastated. Torn. Heartbroken.

I had found my love to heal my emptiness, and that love had wounded me. I had lost everything after a little splash of affection. All that was left was a bundle of memories and her smiling face. There was hardly a moment when I wasn't thinking of her. My pain was becoming deeper and harsher. It ached my heart, and went up to my mind. My headaches became pervasive and intense, which was unbearable. It was no less debilitating, leaving me barely able to stand on my feet, leading me to bed so I could lay there like a corpse. Waiting for the pain to go.

Day after day, the pain became fatal, eating me up. Chest pain, headache, night sweats, and insomnia became my everyday companions. Ruchita could sense what I was going through but could not lessen the pain in any way. Every second, a wave of affection overcame me. My heart was filled with nostalgia and I saw her: smiling dimpled cheeks, hair ruffled by a fine breeze, eyes filled with love and a smile that could win a million hearts. I could smell her, sense her presence. My mind unseeingly was with her, looking for her, distant. I sensed her around me. Or did I? I didn't know who I was talking to. I saw myself desolate and alone. I groaned at the memory, suffering all over again.

"Go away. Go away please. Let me live," I squeaked with deliberate, desperate effort. I struggled with those happy memories because they instilled the feeling of loss even more. Lovely thoughts were hounding me. I could no longer distinguish between reality and illusion, between love and attraction, between life and death.

Ruchita came over with her father to see me one day. Or I must have been hallucinating. But she looked horrified on seeing me. She called my father and told him I needed him. Maybe she did. Maybe this was my imagination too. And then it all went blank.

It was unbearable. The whole thing. How fate could play with me like this. That too twice. When nothing seemed to be working for me, I decided to call Gaurav.

After three rings, he picked up and the moment he said hello, I started sobbing uncontrolledly. I explained everything though my speech kept faltering. He didn't speak for a long time

"It's all destiny, Sanjeev. Not every love story ends in union. You need to grow with this. Most of the people would try to subside it by distracting it with some activities, but since you are a writer, your feelings can be better vented by writing. Even this pain comes to you like a single fine thread of a fabric and when you realize the quantum of the fabric, it makes you sad. Let it be. Pain with this intensity after these years clearly indicates that you are reaching the end of the tunnel. It's like the darkest night happens just before dawn."

"Gaurav, I won't be able do this. It was you who suggested me to go out and meet people. After meeting her, I felt had I have found my soulmate, but didn't know that my fate has something so disastrous for me. I don't know what to do."

There was deafening silence before Gaurav spoke with an assuring tone, "There is only one way to reduce your pain."

"And what's that?"

"We both know bemoaning fate won't do anything. Nor will going to a psychiatrist help you much. The only way I see is for you to write everything down on paper. It's the only way to keep your memory intact on paper, out from your mind and heart. Otherwise your life will be spent recollecting your old times but the sad part would be that the pleasure of remembering would have been taken from you and it will make you sadder day by day."

I didn't know what to say. When I didn't speak for a few minutes, he continued again, "Why don't you shift to my place for a few weeks? I will take sessions with you and in the meantime, if you feel like writing, you can start working on it. Putting down your feelings on paper will be therapeutic."

I nodded mutely.

In the days to come, I shifted to Gaurav's place in C.R. Park. He was kind enough to give me a room and didn't disturb me much. He spent a lot of time with me, listening to every minute detail of my suffering, comforting me.

✿

After having lost so much in Delhi, I couldn't have the heart to continue living here. I shifted base to Mumbai and joined a new job. Before leaving for Mumbai, I dropped a mail to Ruchita.

Hi Ruchita,

I am leaving Delhi and moving to Mumbai with the hope that a new city will help me to move on in my life.

Life changed in many ways after meeting you. You made me smile, gave me a life. But without Shuchi, it's all barren again, the kind of life I wanted to run away from… but it's all the same again.

Thank you for coming into my life and making it worthy, but I don't think I will be able to live here with so many memories. If I continue to live here, I will be drowned under the weight of memories.

I just want to ask you, why it all happened with me. I know you won't have an answer for this, but why me. I just had the splash of happiness over me but its all over in an instant.

I am at loss of words right now. Take care. Will be in touch with you.

Love you.

I left the city without meeting anyone except Gaurav. Vineet and Abhinav tried to reach me, wondering why I was not coming to office. I stopped taking anyone's call.

❀

One day when memories of her started eating me, not having any other options, I opened my laptop, opened a blank Word document and stared at the screen as tears rolled down. I knew that the only way to soothe my mind and heart was to put my feelings on paper, like last time. I typed her last words as the title – 'You are Forever in My Heart.'

Epilogue

The book launch was successful and there were so many questions asked. I had replied to each one politely, keeping a smiling face. In the end, there were selfie sessions in which I participated happily and tried to be a part of the readers' jubilant mood. After signing several hundreds of copies, I returned to the hotel. Ruchita dropped me back to the hotel and hugged me before she left and asked me to promise her that I won't cry, but tears already rolled down my cheeks.

It was an empty room. I sat on my chair and thought about Shuchi again. I knew no matter how happy I looked on the outside, I was empty and alone deep within. I didn't realize for how many hours I sat on the chair, but I woke up with my body aching at having slept in a sitting posture. It was around 2 a.m. when I woke up; my phone had vibrated. I unlocked the phone to be greeted by the wallpaper. It was our last selfie Shuchi had taken by the lakeside, lying under the sky on the green grass. I checked my personal email. There were no new emails except a few promotional mails that I tried to remove so many times so that they stop spamming with their ludicrous promotional offers. Before I could click on the logout button, I refreshed it for some unknown reason absent mindedly and a new mail popped up. It was from Shuchi. Reading the name, I sat up straight. Is it her? I thought, but how could that be possible.

Dear Sanjeev,

It was so wonderful seeing you at your book launch. I might be just someone for you amidst several hundreds of people and I am also not very sure that you even remember me now. You have so many to love you, to get excited for you for I did see how people were jostling among each other just to get a picture with you and get your signature on the novel. Amid all the hustle and bustle, I too had the opportunity to get a picture with you. In fact, I had to push another girl who tried so hard to come into the same picture, but I didn't let her do that. I kept pushing her till the moment someone took a picture of ours. In fact, if I show you the picture, you will be so amazed to see that one of my hands is out of the frame, pushing the other girl. How can she come into our life? Our life?

You know, I got your autograph. Your signature is so lovely and the moment of ecstasy was when you asked me my name and wrote such a lovely, though small, message for me and signed underneath. It's so beautiful. How did you learn this signature?

Love always,
Shuchi Gupta

It wasn't her. It would never happen. She had left me and gone to some other world where she could see me, but I could only remember her. I had made our love story immortal in words as a token of love. I whispered, "You are forever in my heart, Shuchi. I love you."

• • •